THE
DEAD
OF
WINTER

THE
DEAD
OF
WINTER

A Rupert Wilde Mystery

David Stuart Davies

Author Photo Credit: Kathryn White

First edition

ISBN: 978-1-68512-088-7

Cover art by Level Best Designs

This book was professionally typeset on Reedsy.
Find out more at reedsy.com

*To my darling Katie who is my rock, the love of my life
and makes me very nice meals*

Praise for the Works of David Stewart Davies

"(David Stewart Davies)...breathes new life into the traditional British mystery."—Val McDermid

"David Stuart Davies knows how to write and how to twist a knife inside the reader's mind."—Peter James

Prologue

Northern France 1916

'For God's sake go and leave me!'

'Not a chance, old boy.'

'You'll never make it with me.'

'Oh, ye of little faith. We've made it thus far… I thought you were enjoying the old piggyback ride.'

Suddenly the dark, starless sky erupted with fierce yellow light and the ear-splitting thunder of a series of mortar bombs exploding nearby. This was followed by a stuttering fusillade of rifle fire. On the instant Major Rupert Wilde dropped down in the mud, the weight of the young soldier he was carrying on his back forcing him firmly down into the brown squelch. The wet earth pressed against his face, finding entry into his mouth. He gave a moan of dismay but lay prone for some time until the gunfire abated and the sky had darkened once more.

Raising his head slightly, he spat out the mud. 'You OK, Corporal?' he enquired of his companion.

There was a weak muffled response in the affirmative.

'Good man,' murmured Wilde. 'So, let's resume our journey and hope we make it before the Hun have another firework party. Cling on tight!'

With renewed effort, Wilde struggled to his feet, the wounded soldier hanging limply on his back, arms clamped around his neck. Slowly Wilde staggered forward in the blackness towards the British lines. He had forced his mind and body into automatic mode, blanking out all thought and physical sensations He could not allow his thoughts to accept the futility of trying to carry an injured comrade across No Man's Land in the dark or allow his body to feel the pain and strain of his actions. He plodded on like a weary clockwork toy that was slowly winding down.

Again the sky lit up with mortar fire. However, this time it also illuminated a stretch of barbed wire some hundred yards away.

'Nearly home,' Wilde said in a harsh whisper. 'Hold on.'

Some ten laborious minutes later, on reaching the stretch of wire, he laid the exhausted soldier down. 'Now, old lad, we come to the tricky bit,' he said. 'I hope you're up for it.'

The corporal gave an inarticulate response.

Wilde leaned over him and wiped the mud from his face with his sleeve. The soldier's eyes flickered open and his grubby mouth formed itself into a brief smile.

'Glad you're still with us, my friend. Just one last hurdle and then there will be hot tea and fags for us both.'

The corporal nodded.

'Now, let me explain our situation: we're nearly on British territory but we have to get through the wire. The only way is for us to squeeze our way under it. I'm afraid you're going to have to gird up your loins for this last push. Do you think you can do that?'

There was a pause before the corporal replied. 'I'll try, sir' he said, his voice barely more than a whisper.

'Good man. I'll go first and then you try and follow. Burrow down as you slide forward then you can stretch out your arms to me and I'll help to pull you through. Understand?'

'I think so, sir. Don't want to let you down..'

'You won't. Let's hope that luck is on our side.'

Wilde scooped away the mud from beneath the vicious tangle of barbed wire, creating a narrow trench for him to slip down. Slithering slowly beneath the treacherous coils, he gradually made his way forward. At one point his coat became snagged on the wire and in the effort of pulling himself free, his face came in contact with an errant strand which tore into the flesh of his cheek. With gritted teeth, he brushed it away and swore softly. For some moments he lay there, gradually feeling the fatigue and ache in his limbs. He would, he thought, be quite happy to stay here forever, allowing sleep to take him away from this damp and dangerous reality. A burst of gunfire brought him swiftly back from this malaise. With as much energy as he could muster, he squirmed through to the other side.

'Now your turn, corporal,' he called out quietly.

The soldier edged himself forward, gradually managing to make his way halfway under the wire before his uniform jacket becoming snagged on the spikes. 'I can't get loose,' he moaned, wriggling feebly in a vain attempt to release himself. Wilde crawled back under the wire and managed to tug the man's clothing free. 'Now give me your hands and I'll try and pull you through, but for heaven's sake do try and help me.'

'Yes, sir,' came the faint response.

Wilde wriggled his way backwards grasping the corporal's hands and heaving with all his might. The wounded soldier tried hard to help, straining to force himself forward but it was with little effect. Wilde's heart pounded within his chest and he tugged harder to drag the man through, inch by painful inch. It was slow progress, but it was progress.

'Come on, old boy,' Wilde said. 'One last push.'

With a groan, his comrade obeyed, and finally both men had managed to pass under the barrier of barbed wire.

Wilde waited a while for them to get their breath back and then announced: 'Right, old lad, time to be on our way'. With as much energy as he could muster, he heaved his companion to his feet. 'The British trenches are not far away. Do you think you can make it on foot with my help?' he asked.

'I'll give it my best, sir.'

'Good man. That's the ticket. Let's go.'

They hadn't gone but a few feet when there was another burst of gunfire and Wilde felt a searing pain in his shoulder. And just as he realised that he had been hit, he lost consciousness, sinking down once more into the muddy quagmire.

* * *

Gentle indistinguishable sounds whispered in his ear. Gradually they grew louder and then he could make out human voices – speaking low as though they were passing on secrets. Instinctively he opened his eyes. At first his vision was cloudy; there was no colour to this world that he had conjured into view. It was a grey blur filled with faint shadows and then imperceptibly the images sharpened. Things came into focus and gradually vivid colour filtered into the scene. A face appeared close to his. It was a woman's face. Bright, warm brown eyes. Smooth cheeks. A hint of lipstick on lips which softened into a smile. 'Welcome back to the land of the living,' she said. The voice was gentle, sweet, and caring; the voice of an angel.

He struggled to sit up, but as he did so his vision blurred again. He groaned.

'Not so fast, soldier,' said the woman, laying a gentle hand on his and easing him back onto the pillow. 'You've got to give it a bit of time before you can start being active. You've a nasty wound there.' She smiled again. It was a very nice smile, Wilde thought.

'Where am I?'

'You are at a casualty clearing station near Hazeebrouk.'

Wilde paused for a moment, his mind still fuzzy. 'You're a nurse.'

The woman smiled again and added a small chuckle. 'Oh, you're a bright one.'

'Sorry, just a bit slow at the moment.'

'That's understandable, Major. You were brought here with a bullet wound and complete exhaustion. By a miracle, the bullet just missed the subclavian artery.'

'But I'm all right now?'

'You will be in time. You'll need to convalesce for a while and no doubt because of your bravery the authorities will grant you a nice little leave in London before you return to your duties.'

'Bravery?'

'Yes, for saving the life of one of your battalion—bringing him back from the enemy lines.'

'Oh, yes.' The memory gradually seeped back into his brain. 'Corporal White. How is he?'

'Actually, he's in better shape than you. He should be up and about in a few days, little the worse for wear, thanks to you.'

It was Wilde's turn to grin. 'At least the blighter made it.'

'He made it all right, with your help. Now you need to rest. A good sleep, eh?'

'Anything, you say nurse.' Wilde turned on his side, the one with the good shoulder, and closed his eyes. This bloody war, he thought as sleep began to encroach on him. This bloody war. When it's all over I am going to live the sedentary life of a gentleman. No more danger and excitement for me.

Chapter One

August 1919

Detective Inspector Johnny Ferguson took a sip of scotch and then stared over the rim of his glass at Major Rupert Wilde, his good friend from their time at Oxford. Wilde was reclining on a chaise longue, sheathed in a fetching red silk dressing gown. He also had a drink in hand but he hadn't touched it. With his head lolling back he seemed to be preoccupied by the intricate coving that ran along the edge of the ceiling in his London flat. It was a face that could have belonged to one of the Roman Caesars: it was long and thin, with high cheekbones and in possession of a prominent nose. It was this nose, aquiline and slightly crooked, that robbed Wilde of the description of 'handsome'. In truth, his friend thought that he had the face of a poet rather than a warrior.

Ferguson mused that Wilde had not yet recovered the bloom in his cheeks or lost the gaunt features that he had inherited as a result of four years service in France. It seemed to him that the war had drained some of the spirit out of the man. He knew that he had been wounded in the shoulder and awarded the George Cross for an act 'of the greatest heroism or for most conspicuous courage in circumstance of extreme danger' as the dedication had it. It was an experience that Wilde was very reluctant to talk about but the inspector could tell that it had a great effect on Rupert's character and outlook on life.

Ferguson brought to mind the blithe fellow he had spent many happy hours with at university. Then he was full of fun, bright and adventurous – a lively and witty companion. To be fair, there were still flashes of the old Wilde in his demeanour, but Ferguson realised that it would take a while for him to shrug off the effects of the time he had spent in the trenches fighting the Hun and witnessing the horrors of that bloody conflict. A kind of dull shadow now hovered over his character.

He considered that phrase: 'still flashes of the old Wilde'. Well, Ferguson had seen some of these in his recent investigation—the case of Lady Dobney's missing diamond tiara. As his sergeant had been down with the dreaded Spanish flu, the inspector had enlisted his old friend, who he knew was at a loose end and twiddling his inactive thumbs, to assist him in an unofficial capacity with the investigation. He thought that a demanding intellectual challenge would help in some way to revive 'the old Wilde'. Something to get him active again and involved in society. However, he had not reckoned on the brilliant way that Rupert had led him to the solution of the mystery and the recovery of the tiara. He had solved the case deftly, with panache and virtually on his own. Wilde had demonstrated some remarkably perceptive sleuthing powers that had both surprised and impressed him. His friend seemed to be in his element playing bloodhound and it was gratifying to see the spark of enthusiasm in his bright blue eyes once more. However, after the case was over and the culprit exposed, the spark had faded away again.

'A penny for them?' Ferguson said quietly.

Wilde pursed his lips and casually brushed away the comma of blonde hair that crested his forehead. 'I shouldn't waste your money, old bean. There's nothing going on in this dull brain box of mine worth you shelling out the shekels for.'

'Well, I'd like to make a toast to you, Mr Sherlock Holmes Wilde for a very neat piece of detective work.'

'It was elementary,' said Wilde seriously and then gave a sudden grin, raising his glass.

'It was far from that. The way you demolished the solicitor's alibi and located the secret hiding place of the tiara was a bloomin' tour de force.'

'My blushes, old boy.' His eyes flashed with humour.

'Seriously, Rupert, have you ever thought about joining the police? Scotland Yard could do with a smart chap like you.'

Wilde gave a mock shudder. 'What, put on a uniform again? No fear! I think I've had enough of all that palaver.'

'With your brains and my recommendations, I'm sure we could get you into plain clothes in quick sticks.'

'Plain clothes? What would my tailor say?' Another brief smile.

'I mean it, Rupert.'

'Oh, and so do I. Quite honestly, Johnny, the thought of rules and regulations, writing reports, adhering to the scruples of legal convention would drive me up the wall—further up the bally wall than I am now. I need freedom, not the restrictions that being a member of the police force would bring.'

'Oh, it's not so bad.'

'I can see that it suits you, right enough, and I'm pleased for you, but while solving a crime is quite appealing, the process of carrying it out while wearing the straitjacket of officialdom would stifle me.'

'Well, I suppose you could set yourself up as a private detective. That way you'd be your own man.'

Rupert shook his head again. 'Private tecs in fiction like good old Sherlock, Sexton Blake, and that lot do very well for strange and exciting cases landing in their lap, mysteries that challenge the intellect and fire up the weary blood cells, but that's fiction. In reality, all these poor chaps get are cases of infidelity, lost cats, and missing spouses. I'd probably get more thrills directing traffic.'

'Is that what you are after, excitement?'

Wilde took a sip of whisky. 'In a way, I suppose I am. Not the sort I got in the war with good men, soldiers under my command, dropping dead at my feet and trying to survive in the cold and the mud while attempting to remain sane and rational. That wasn't excitement, it was just action and reaction prompted by fear.'

'Believe me, Rupert, I understand. So now you have your feet firmly planted on the pavement of civvy street, what exactly do you intend to do?'

'I am not sure, but I can tell you I am in no hurry to make decisions or take uncertain roads. Something will turn up, I'm sure. I'm a great believer in fate. At the moment I want to get my head and body into gear again and then take life as it comes. My wound has healed nicely, thank you very much, but I'm not so sure about my mind. I need time to wash away the scenes of death and destruction and for a kind of amnesia to take their place. Then I can think about the future. I am lucky to have a very comfortable fortune to cushion me thanks to my dear but sadly departed pa, so I can afford to take all the time in the world.'

'Well, my friend, I wish you luck.'

With this statement, the two men drained their glasses.

* * *

That night, as Wilde lay in bed thinking about his conversation with Johnny, he began to examine his responses to his old friend's suggestion that he should take up detective work as a career. Perhaps it had not been such a bad idea after all. However, he still considered that joining the police force with all its rules and rigid structures was out of the question. He had experienced some of the institutional hurdles one had to jump over in order to progress with a case when he'd worked with Johnny on the Dobney affair: paperwork, warrants, strict procedures. Most of the time these starchy regulations simply erected irritating obstacles to getting the job done effectively and efficiently. Rupert had already decided that whatever occupation he took up now that he was out of the army, he was not going to be controlled by such hindrances. He had to be his own man, free to make his own decisions without being beholden to anyone but himself. Now, if he was a private investigator, he certainly would have that sort of freedom. But would the work interest him? Would it present him with the kind of challenges he would find stimulating? He had no desire to sit in hotel lobbies on the lookout for an errant husband escorting a tarty blonde up to his room. Such mundane endeavours would be an anathema to him. He shuddered at the thought. In the end, as tiredness began its gentle ambush on his senses, he decided to forget about playing Sherlock Holmes for the time being. He was sure that Time and Fate would sort things out. With a yawn, he turned on his good shoulder and drifted off to sleep.

CHAPTER ONE

***

He wasn't to know it at the time, but two weeks later, a new beginning for Rupert Wilde was about to present itself. It was one of those late summer days where the sky was a cloudless blue, the air was warm and the trees had not yet begun to don their autumn plumage. He was making his way back to his flat in Chancery Court in Kensington when, as he was passing by an alleyway, he heard what sounded like cries for help. He gazed down the gloomy, narrow passage and saw the silhouettes of three animated figures. Sensing something was wrong, he moved nearer, and he saw that there were two men attacking a third.

'Don't like those odds,' he murmured, breaking into a sprint.

One of the men observed his approach. 'Bleedin' hell, here comes the cavalry,' he cried, his voice aiming at bravado but not quite hitting the target. He turned on Wilde, pulling a knife out of his belt and thrusting it forward towards him. 'Beat it or it will be the worse for you,' he growled.

Wilde quickly deflected the ruffian's arm with a hard blow and followed this up by a swift uppercut to the chin. With a moan, the fellow crumpled to the ground. His associate, observing the actions of this new combatant, gave a yelp of fear and took flight. As did the knife-wielding assailant once he'd scrambled to his feet.

Wilde turned his attention to the young man lying on the ground. He possessed swarthy features and was dressed in a pale linen suit. He was clutching a leather briefcase in both his hands.

'How are you? Did they harm you?' asked Wilde.

'I am fine and most grateful, sir,' came the faint reply.

'Can you get to your feet?'

'With your assistance, I am sure that I can do so.'

Wilde helped the man into an erect posture. He now saw that he was a young Indian.

'They were after my briefcase,' he said, clutching it to his chest. 'It was a present from my father. It is empty apart from my sandwiches – but I was not about to let those blackguards take it from me.'

'You did well.'

'Not well enough. If it had not been for you, they would have stolen it.'

Wilde ignored the compliment. 'Are you hurt?' he asked.

The young man grinned broadly, his teeth gleaming brightly in the darkness. 'Only my pride. A little stiff, a few bruises but I will survive and I have my briefcase.' He patted it affectionately.

'I live close by, come along with me and partake of a reviving drink. A whisky and soda perhaps.'

'Oh, no, sir. I am a Hindu and we are not permitted alcohol.'

'A cup of tea then?'

'Ah, that would be most kind. I am sure that would certainly help to revive me.'

A short time later the young Indian was seated on Wilde's sofa with a cup of Earl Grey and a china plate containing a muffin. Wilde sat opposite him, cradling a whisky and soda in both hands.

'You are most gracious, Mr...' said the young man, brushing crumbs away from his lips.

'Wilde. Rupert Wilde. And you are...?

'I am Kishen Chabra, at your service, sir.' He gave a deferential nod of the head.

'Your English is very good.'

Kishen bowed his head. 'I thank you. I have been in England for fifteen years now. I was educated at one of your public schools, Rugby, and I recently graduated from Oxford.'

'Oh, really, which college?'

'Corpus Christi.'

'Ah, I was at Balliol.'

Kishen beamed. 'So, in a sense, we are fellow old boys.'

Wilde nodded with a smile. 'I guess we are. Tell me what happened just now with those ruffians?'

Kishen shrugged. 'I was making my way along the street minding my own business when they approached me and demanded that I handed over my briefcase and my wallet. Of course, I refused and before I knew what was happening, they had dragged me down the alley and began attacking me, but I held on to my briefcase because it means so much to me. And then you came along like one of those knights in medieval tales, like Sir Walter Scott's Ivanhoe, and rescued me.'

Wilde chuckled. 'I've never been compared to a medieval knight before, but I'll take the compliment. Why is the briefcase so precious to you? I can see it is a fine one, beautiful leather, but there must be more to it than that. You say your father gave it to you.'

Kishen nodded. 'On my visit to India before I started my studies at Oxford. It was the last time I saw him alive. He died in my second year. I am now an orphan.'

'Sorry to hear that, old boy. I can see how the briefcase has a special place in your heart.'

'Indeed, it has great sentimental value. And you very kindly helped me to hold on to it.'

'So what are you doing with yourself now you have brushed off the dust of Oxford?'

'Ah, Mr Wilde, that is a moot point. I am attempting to find employment but I am failing miserably. It seems that positions both high and low have no requirement for an Indian graduate of History and Philosophy. I have applied to businesses, educational establishments, even a tramcar company but have been rejected by all. I fear that it may be because of my colour. They do not want a young brown person as part of their workforce. I am sorry to say that.'

Wilde refrained from comment but his instinct told him that unfortunately the young man was most likely correct in this assumption.

'To be honest with you, Mr Wilde, I am growing desperate now. My savings are rapidly dwindling. If I do not find employment in the next month I shall have to return to India. My uncle has offered me a job as a clerk in the factory that he owns in Jaipur. It is a generous offer but a lowly position without intellectual challenges. And I really do not want to go back to India. I like it here. I must admit I feel more at home in this country than I do in India. I like England and its way of life. Rule Britannia, I say.' He smiled again, his face lighting up with enthusiasm.

Wilde placed his whisky glass on the table and extracted a silver cigarette case from his pocket. 'I suppose you don't smoke either,' he said proffering the case to his guest.

Kishen shook his head. 'I do not, sir.'

'You are a clean living boy, aren't you?'

'I endeavour to be so.'

'How would you like to work for me?'

Kishen's eyes widened in surprise. 'For you? In what capacity...?'

'Well, I need an assistant. Someone to look after me. See to my clothes, cook a few simple meals, deal with the paperwork, help organise my life.'

'You mean like a servant.'

'Servant sounds a bit harsh. I have no intention of you bowing and scraping like some old family retainer. I prefer the term *assistant*.'

'Oh, I am not upset by the word *servant*. In India, this is a respected role, especially if one is serving someone of importance.'

Wilde laughed. 'Well, we can knock that notion on the head for a start. I am certainly no one of any great importance.'

'But you were a major in the army.'

'How d'you know that?'

'I saw letters in the silver tray in the hall addressed to you and there is that picture of you on the mantelpiece with a group of soldiers.'

'Perceptive little devil, aren't you?'

'I use my eyes.'

'An admirable trait. I like that. So, what do you say? Are you up for giving it a go? I suggest a month's trial to see how we rub along. We may not be at all compatible and then again ...'

'To be offered any kind of employment is very tempting, I must admit.'

'If you want time to think it over.'

'No, no. Procrastination is a weakness. I will say yes.'

'Good man. We can settle financial terms later – but I can assure you that your remuneration will be greater than anything on offer from a tram car company.'

Kishen laughed.

'So,' said Wilde, 'you can move in here as soon as you like. There is a bedroom with a private bath at the rear of the premises and a spacious lumber room which I'll clear out and fix up as your private quarters—if that will suit.'

'It will suit most admirably,' said Kishen, smiling broadly.

Chapter Two

Aubrey Sinclair examined the contents of the envelope he had just opened at the breakfast table. 'What is the date today?' he asked sharply, the request emerging rather like a peevish demand.

His wife glanced up from the *Daily Telegraph*. 'My paper says it is October the eighteenth, 1919,' she said crisply. 'Why do you ask?'

Sinclair waved a sheet of writing paper before him. 'It seems that Christmas has come early this year.'

'What are you talking about?'

'We've been invited to spend Christmas with the Markhams. It seems your friend Lady Julia is keen for us to share their festive *bonhomie* at Pelham House in the wilds of Norfolk.'

'Really? Let me see.'

Sinclair passed over the handwritten message to his wife,

'Why, it's going to be a house party,' she said with enthusiasm. 'It sounds rather jolly.'

'You think so? Old Algernon's a bit of a stuffed shirt and Julia…well, she's a bit dipsy.'

'What's our alternative? Booking into one of those mausoleums of a hotel for two days while the servants creep around us and we sleep in draughty bedrooms.'

'We could always stay at home.'

'And you'll cook…?'

Sinclair gave a heavy sigh. 'Put like that, I suppose it would be a bit of a change.'

'Indeed. And you never know it could be fun.'

'I'll not hold my breath.'

'If only you would,' she said, adding brightly, 'anyway it's settled. I'll write today accepting their kind invitation. At least a house party will give me the chance to talk to someone else over Christmas lunch rather than you.'

* * *

When Jonquil Callow was in creative mode, he was not conscious of the outside world. He slipped into a bubble of isolation where only ideas and words had any relevance in his life. He was working on another poem when the postman called that morning. He knocked with some force on the door of Callow's flat but received no response and was on the verge giving up when he decided to give it one more try—with even greater force.

In his tiny sitting room, lost in creation, Callow was hunched on the sofa, notepad in hand, hovering over the choice of adjective to give greater mood and pertinence to the line, when finally the blows being administered to his front door penetrated the bubble. With a sigh of irritation, reluctantly he dropped the pad and pencil on the sofa and went to answer the door.

'Thought you were out,' said the postman with some sarcasm, handing over a small parcel and two letters.

'Well, I wasn't quite here,' Callow replied mysteriously before closing the door. He opened the parcel first and beamed with delight at the contents. There were six author copies of his latest anthology of poems, *Amber in the Afternoon*. He flicked through the pages, emitting a satisfied purr as he did so. It really was a smart looking volume and the work within was all his own. Could this be the tome that would bring him to the attention of some of the major critics? He really hoped so. He knew he had greatness within him, if only someone influential would spot it.

The first envelope he opened contained a letter from the bank informing him that his account was seriously overdrawn and they would be obliged if he would make an appointment to see the manager so that this matter could be discussed and rectified.

'Rats,' he snarled, somewhat unpoetically.

The second envelope held a letter from Lady Julia Markham inviting him to a Christmas house party. Callow frowned heavily at the prospect, but no sooner had this thought entered his head than another replaced it. Lady Julia had been kind and, indeed, helpful to him. It was she who had introduced him to Mr Belvedere of Bronski Press, which led to his latest slim volume of verse being published. And a house party – who knew what other useful contacts could be made at such an event. Lady Julia was a bit fluttery but he would be foolish to dismiss the invitation out of hand. Indeed, very swiftly, he came to think that he wouldn't dismiss it at all. He would waste no time in replying to the invitation in the affirmative.

* * *

Stella Bond felt wretched. She knew important decisions had to be made and no matter which path she chose it would change her life forever and not in a good way. Or at least not in the way she had anticipated less than a year ago. What made the wretchedness worse was the realisation that she was partly to blame for her dilemma. She had followed her heart rather than…If only she had not been so stupid.

However, Stella was conscious that one could not live one's life considering the 'if onlies.' She was bright and independent enough to know one must accept the status quo—even if it is not the status quo she desired – and work with that.

And it was business today so for the moment she must concentrate on that. At least she still was able to continue with her profession. She entered the gallery with her briefcase ready to peruse and assess the collection of Italian miniatures on behalf of the curator. It was only at lunch, taken in a small tea room near to the gallery that she had a chance to check through her morning post that she had snatched up and thrust into her briefcase before leaving her tiny flat that morning. There were three items: two letters from friends and the invitation from Lady Julia Markham to 'join in the fun of a Christmas House Party.' She knew that this was coming and she would accept of course.

She had to, but it would be with little enthusiasm. As she finished her chicken salad, the phrase 'if only' wandered into her mind again.

* * *

'It just won't do Hargreaves,' Bertram John Silverside looked up from the file on his desk that he had been perusing when Alfred Hargreaves had entered his office.

Hargreaves pursed his lips but kept silent.

'You know what I'm talking about, don't you?'

'I think so,' replied Hargreaves, his voice barely above a whisper, his eyes examining his shoes.

'You think so,' said Silverside, his voice barely below a bellow. He stabbed the file with his chubby finger. 'In the last month under your stewardship production has fallen by almost twenty percent. It will not do, Hargreaves. I tell you, it will not do.'

'There's been a lot of illness, sir: Spanish flu and the usual winter coughs and colds. The absenteeism has been above average.'

'Has it, by Jove? And what have you done about it?'

Hargreaves was frightened of admitting that he had done nothing about it and so he remained silent.

'You are the senior foreman on the shop floor, Hargreaves. I expect you to deal with such matters. If there is a hole where a peg should be, you find another ruddy peg. How can we keep up production if we have a row of empty pegs? Do you understand?'

Hargreaves nodded.

'Right then, I'll give you a fortnight to sort this matter out. I want my figures up again. Production at full pelt. If you are not capable of carrying out your duties, you may well find that you end up as a missing peg as well. D'you get my drift?'

'I do, Mr Silverside. Thank you, sir.' Hargreaves retreated towards the door, walking backwards until he turned awkwardly and departed in haste.

Silverside shook his head and sighed.

The phone rang and he lifted the receiver.

'There's a personal call for you, Mr Silverside,' said his secretary in a clipped efficient tone.

'Who is it?'

'Algernon Markham.'

Silverside hesitated for a minute, sighed again, and then said: 'All right. Put him through.'

There was a crackle on the line and then a tinny voice said: 'Bertie?'

'Algy. How nice to hear your voice. How are you and your lovely lady?'

'We're fine.'

'Good, good. So what can I do for you? Is it about your paintings again? I certainly will find time soon to come and visit and give them the once over. It's just that we're...rather busy at the moment. One or two problems on the production line.'

'Well, it's not totally about the paintings—but it's good news that you are still interested.'

'Yes.' There was an air of reluctance in the response.

'Well, actually the reason I'm ringing is that Julia and I are having a Christmas House party—Christmas Eve through to Boxing Day and we'd love you to be part of the throng.'

'Throng? How many are you expecting?'

'Oh, not many: around six or so. We thought it would be fun if you could come along and, of course, it will give you the opportunity to see the paintings.'

'Of course. Good idea. Lovely of you to invite me. Can I take a rain check on this—I don't have my diary with me at present,' he said, tapping his diary with his forefinger.'

'Certainly. That is no problem.' Markham seemed disappointed.

'I'll get back to you before the end of next week. Is that acceptable?'

'Yes, yes, of course. Thank you.'

'Well, must get on. Busy, busy.'

'Of course. Look forward to hearing from you.'

'Bye Algy.'

'Cheerio.'

Bertram John Silverdale sat back in his chair with one of his customary sighs. He reached out for his diary and opened it at the week covering the Christmas period. The entries were blank. Silverside pursed his lips. 'Ah well...I suppose...' he said at length with little enthusiasm.

* * *

After he'd parked his car in front of Pelham House, despite the sleeting rain, he remained for some time gazing at the building. He had visited the venerable old pile many times since he had taken up medical practice in the village—Lady Julia and husband Algernon had become regular patients—but he never lost the sense of wonder at the house, admiring the beautiful architecture and symmetry of its structure and appearance. It was aging badly now and was becoming unmanageable as a domestic dwelling, with so many rooms to heat and maintain, a labyrinth of winding corridors, and no doubt a crippling upkeep. Locke was convinced that when the present owners passed away, the house would either crumble into ruins or be taken over by the state as an historic entity. Either way, it would be a pity. It needed to be lived in with someone with very deep pockets who could restore it fully to its former glory.

The wind and sleet increased suddenly and turning up his collar Doctor Locke rushed towards the entrance of the house. Once inside, Boldwood, the butler, led him to the sitting room where Lady Julia was resting on a sofa quietly reading a novel. She looked up at his entrance. Locke was a lean good-looking man in his thirties, with keen eyes and a generous smile which often charmed his female patients, including Julia. Similarly, the doctor found her a pleasant woman but with a nervous disposition which partly was responsible for her high blood pressure. On testing it, he found it was particularly high on this occasion. On receiving this news, Lady Julia smiled gently and seemed more amused than concerned.

'I'm afraid I would advise that we increase the medication in an attempt to stabilise your condition and then with a bit of luck reduce your level.'

Lady Julia smiled sweetly. 'Whatever you say. You're the doctor.'

'And how are you in yourself?' asked Locke tentatively.

'Don't be coy, Doctor. Are you asking if I'm still having my gloomy days? Well, I don't. Your special pills have cheered me up no end. I feel like a new woman.' She giggled and stroked Locke's hand. 'I don't know what I'd do without you. I thank you so much.'

Somewhat embarrassed by the intimacy of the gesture, Locke gently removed his hand and rose to leave. 'I'm glad to hear it, Lady Julia. If only all my patients were as grateful.' He smiled uneasily and left the room.

Before departing Pelham House, Locke visited Algernon Markham in his study to give him an update regarding his wife's medication. It was a cosy chamber with a blazing fire and soft lighting which allowed the oak panelling to fade into the shadows.

'Certainly, Julia is much like her old self again,' said Markham. 'Those antidepressants you've prescribed seem to be doing wonders. Of course, we're still both concerned about the cost of maintaining this house. It is a real worry for her. It is really draining our resources, but no doubt we'll survive.'

'Indeed, I am sure you will. And how are things with you, sir?' asked Locke.

'Oh, I'm fine at the moment, thank you. No sign of the gout, I'm glad to say. In fact, nothing to complain about at all.'

'Very good. In that case, I'll be on my way, then.'

'No, no, don't go just yet. How about a snifter and a game of chess, Doctor,' said Markham.

It was the usual routine when Locke visited the house. Markham struck Locke as rather a lonely man, rattling around in this large house with only his wife for company. A glass of whisky and a game of chess was a pleasant diversion. The doctor was happy to accept the invitation for he too was rather a solitary figure having only settled in the village just six months earlier from his native Scotland, with only his patients as acquaintances at the moment.

Markham poured the drinks—single malts—and set up the chessboard. 'How is it that a young well set up fellow like yourself has no wife,' he asked before taking a sip of his scotch.

'Young?' Locke smiled. 'I'm nearly forty.' The smile faded. 'I had a wife but she died. Cancer.'

'Oh, I'm so very sorry. I'd no idea...'

'That's okay—why should you? But her death was one of the reasons I moved south. It's not good for a doctor if he can't even cure his own wife's illness. Not good for trade, you understand.' He gave a bitter grin. 'I came here for a fresh start and I think it's working.'

'You have no other family?'

'I have a brother herding sheep in Australia and a sister nursing in Ireland. We keep in touch by the occasional letter but the distances mean we never meet.'

'It seems that you could do with a girlfriend.'

'Oh, really. Have you anyone in mind?'

Markham shook his head. 'At the moment, I'm afraid not.' A sudden thought struck him. 'What are you doing at Christmas?'

'Christmas? Oh, I've not even thought about that.'

'How would you like to spend it with us? We're having a little house party – just a few guests and you'd be very welcome.'

Locke hesitated. 'I don't really know...'

'Oh, do come. It will be better than sitting alone in your cottage tackling a solitary turkey drumstick, with no one to pull a cracker. And we could always manage to squeeze in a game of chess.'

Locke grinned. 'Put like that... well, it does sound tempting.'

'Good then it's settled. You are on the guest list.'

'Well, you are very kind.'

'Nothing of the sort. I am sure you will enjoy yourself. It promises to be a very jolly affair.'

Chapter Three

Christmas Eve 1919

The December day was drawing to its close as Rupert Wilde's bright red roadster negotiated the narrow Norfolk lanes with reckless abandon. The grim, grey winter sky, which threatened snow, was glimpsed above the tall hedges as the car skimmed along, its headlights carving two shafts of yellow into the gloom ahead. Stars were gradually making their pin pricks of light visible in the darkening canopy and a pale crescent moon peeped hesitantly from behind a bank of ragged clouds.

'I am very keen to reach our destination before it gets really dark,' said Rupert Wilde, as he swung the vehicle around another tight bend, with an unnerving screech of tyres. 'These roads are confusing enough in the daylight…' His companion, Kishen Chabra, sitting bolt upright beside him and gripping the edge of the leather passenger seat, nodded vigorously. 'I shall certainly be glad when we get there also, sir,' he said, closing his eyes once more as Wilde shot across another set of hidden crossroads without a glance in either direction.

'Kishen, I've told you before, do not call me sir. We agreed on this from the start. You are not my servant, my khitmagar. You are my assistant and in other respects my equal. I am Rupert. Got that.'

'But you are also my employer.'

'That is neither here nor there. It is Rupert. Rupert. Got that.'

Kishen nodded vigorously. 'Yes, sir…er, Rupert.'

'Good man.'

Wilde took another bend at breakneck speed.

'It was awfully kind of Aunt Julia to invite us to her jolly Christmas bash,' he said. 'Otherwise, we'd be spending it on our lonesome in the flat in London. It will be fun for you to see how the English upper classes make fools of themselves at Christmas.'

'You forget that I went to Oxford University.'

'Ah, yes.'

Wilde had at first been undecided whether to accept the invitation from his aunt whom he had not seen for some time. Initially, the thought of being cooped up in the mausoleum of a house with a group of strangers had no appeal to him at all. However, Aunt Julia had assured him in her letter that 'the guests are in the main jolly artistic types whom I'm sure you'll get on with like that proverbial house on fire,' and so, on reflection, he had reconsidered the invitation. He told himself that it was time he made an effort to get back into the swing of society now that the war was over. Four years away in France had meant that he was out of touch with many of his social contacts; indeed he had lost a number of them in the mud of the trenches.

In the end, it had been Kishen who had persuaded him to change his mind. The most astute of fellows, Kishen had very quickly realised that his master was having grave difficulty settling down to civilian life and that there was a streak of sadness about his character now that not only gave the twenty-nine-year-old bachelor a kind of seriousness and maturity beyond his years, but also a tendency to suffer occasional bouts of melancholy causing him to seek isolation for a time. A Christmas house party could well be the very thing not only to to raise his spirits but also revive his appetite for a full social ife.

Wilde himself knew that in order to conquer his dark moods he had to involve himself in the whirl of humanity once more. The world was on the brink of a bright new decade and he was determined to embrace it with all the vim and vigour he could muster. Indirectly, Kishen's apparent enthusiasm for the festive gathering at his aunt's place, Pelham House, in the fens of Norfolk, had made Wilde realise that this was a wonderful opportunity for him to re-join the human race.

'Thar she blows!' he cried, raising one hand from the steering wheel as the car began to make its way up a steep incline, a rare feature in the flat Norfolk countryside. Kishen sat up in his seat, his face aglow with excitement. He followed Wilde's gesture and saw some distance away the silhouette of a large house, the lights of its windows seeming to his imagination like welcoming Christmas illuminations.

'Gracious. It is like a castle. No doubt Robin Hood slept there,' said Kishen.

'No doubt he did, along with Maid Marian, lucky boy,' chuckled Wilde. 'Well, it is an ancient old pile, dating back to the sixteenth century, I think.'

'Oh, early seventeen hundreds, I should say. It is very much in the Baroque style made popular by John Vanbrugh.'

Wilde passed his companion a swift glance.

Kishen grinned. 'As you know, I studied History at university.'

'Of course. You have many hidden depths, Kishen, old chap. I like that. Well, we're nearly there. I haven't been here since I was a tadpole. A short-trousered waif. It's a house one could easily get lost in. I wonder if I'll remember its geography.'

'If not, I have brought a ball of twine with me.'

Wilde grinned.

'The upkeep of such a place must cost a fortune,' observed Kishen.

'It does, and I gather that dear old Aunt Julia and her relatively new husband are finding things a bit tough at the moment.'

'Relatively new husband?'

'Tied the knot about four years ago. He's her third.'

Kishen gave a gentle whistle.

'She's a lady who needs a man on her arm. There is a vein of insecurity in her nature.'

Moments later Wilde was driving past the gateposts of Pelham House and down the curving drive towards the front of the building. It was quite dark now but there was electric lighting around the portico. Snow was beginning to fall.

Wilde jumped out of the car and grabbed his valise from the back seat. On cue the door of Pelham House opened and two liveried servants emerged, followed by the stately form of the butler Boldwood whom Wilde remembered from twenty years ago. He was still as erect and of a commanding demeanour as before, although the hair, what there was left of it, had turned white and the stern features were now heavily lined.

'Master Wilde isn't it, sir?' he said in sonorous tones.

'It is, although I haven't been addressed as such for decades. 'Good to see you, Boldwood, old chap.' Wilde just managed to stop himself from calling him Boldy as he had referred to him behind his back in the old days.

'These fellows will see to your luggage and have it taken to your rooms.'

'Good-oh. Here's the open sesame to the boot.' He lobbed the key to Boldwood who caught it deftly and then passed it to one of the servants.

'Her ladyship is in the drawing room with some of the other guests. Would you like me to show you through?'

'Very well, if you'll also see to my associate, Mr Chabra here. He'll no doubt welcome a cup of tea and a rest after the hair-raising ride I've just given him.'

Boldwood nodded. It was an eloquent gesture which indicated that all would be seen to. Like a game of follow my leader, Wilde, Kishen and the two burdened lackeys trooped into the grand hall of Pelham House. Standing near the bottom of the curving staircase was a tall, beautifully decorated Christmas tree, illuminated with a myriad of sparkling lights which gave a vibrant aura to the gloomy hallway.

Wilde stood before it and smiled. 'Now it really feels like Christmas. What do you think, Kishen?'

'It is most impressive—a rival for the one in Windsor Castle.'

'Indeed. Whoever decorated it did a beautiful job.'

'Lady Julia supervised the operation, sir,' said Boldwood solemnly. 'The servants obeyed her instructions to the letter.'

Wilde chuckled. 'I bet they did.'

* * *

Some moments later, Boldwood opened the doors of the drawing room and announced the arrival of Major Rupert Wilde. The room was warm with a log fire in the grate; there was the low hum of conversation and the gentle clinking of crystal champagne glasses.

A plumpish lady in a shimmering pink cocktail gown rushed forward and threw her arms around Rupert. 'Oh, I am so glad you could make it, my dear boy,' she cooed and planted a wet kiss on his cheek, leaving behind a faint smear of lipstick.

Lady Julia Markham was a woman of some sixty years. It was a fact that she did not admit to anyone, not even herself. When she looked in the mirror, with one eye closed, she still saw the lissom twenty-five-year-old beauty she had once been. She was used to quoting that old bit of Shakespeare: 'Age cannot wither her, nor custom stale her infinite variety.' She was fully convinced that these sentiments applied to her.

Wilde had not seen his aunt for two years and he noticed quite a change in her appearance. She had put on a few pounds in weight and, despite her smiling countenance and carefully applied makeup, her face spoke of strain and worry. The result, no doubt, of her concerns over money. He knew the cost of maintaining Pelham House was an immense drain on her dwindling fortune. He sensed that her rather forced jollity was a kind of emotional camouflage.

Wilde was fond of his aunt, although he accepted that she was somewhat foolish, often over-emotional, and a little neurotic. But she had charm and some of her mannerisms reminded him of her sister, his mother, Sarah. Although she had not been as pretty as Julia, she had possessed a fine brain and was a wonderful mother.

'Lovely to be here, darling, and so grateful to be invited. London can be rather lonely at Yuletide,' he said cheerily.

Wilde was conscious of a figure hovering close to Lady Julia. It was Algernon Markham, his aunt's third husband. He was a tall man, some fifteen years younger than his wife, in possession of broad shoulders, and an open and handsome face, but somehow to Wilde he always seemed to cut a mysterious figure, a shadow rather than substance. He was, Wilde thought, an iceberg of a man. One only glimpsed the part of his character which he was prepared to share with the world; there was much more below the surface of the water that remained unseen. Markham stepped forward, his right arm extended, and the two men shook hands.

'Good to see you, Rupert. I must say you're looking well. The colour has returned to the cheeks. You were a bit of a skeleton last time I saw you.'

Wilde smiled. 'It's all due to Kishen, my assistant, he's been feeding me up and insisting I take a long walk each day.'

Markham nodded. 'Well, it's working.'

Lady Julia took Wilde's arm. 'Come along, dear boy, let me get you a drink and then I'll introduce you to our guests. We're all here now apart from Doctor Locke who warned me he would be late. He's comparatively new to the area. He took over old Poulson's practice. You remember him?'

'Vaguely,' Wilde replied.

There were five other guests in the room, each with champagne glass in hand; Rupert Wilde was paraded before them.

'This is Aubrey Sinclair, the playwright, and his wife Sonia Lane – *the* Sonia Lane.'

Sinclair was a small, neat fellow with a thin moustache and small piggy eyes; his dark hair, glistening with oil, was combed back from the face in a severe fashion. Wilde thought he had the appearance and demeanour of an aggressive, diminutive sergeant major rather than a flamboyant playwright. He tapped Wilde on the elbow in greeting. 'I gather you've been in the war ...'

Wilde nodded.

'Good show.'

Not really. Bloody awful, actually, thought Wilde. Instinctively he touched his wounded shoulder while images of dead soldiers ensnared on the barbed wire in the mud of Flanders flashed briefly into his mind. However, he kept his own counsel.

Sonia Lane held out her hand and Wilde kissed it. Of course he recognised her: the famous actress. 'So pleased to meet you,' he said warmly. 'I saw you at the Adelphi in *What Matters is Murder* a few years ago when I was home on leave.'

Sonia Lane gave a light laugh. 'Oh, that old thing,' she said.

23

'Careful dear,' said her husband, rather tartly. 'Remember, I wrote that old thing.'

Sonia laughed again. It was all rather theatrical.

Wilde assumed that she was now somewhere in her early forties and while she remained an attractive woman, the signs of ageing were subtly making their presence felt on her striking features. She must have been an absolute stunner in her youth, mused Wilde, while at the same time wondering how the little stiff-backed playwright had managed to snare her.

The other three people in the room were next on Lady Julia's parade of introductions.

'This is Jonquil Callow, a very promising poet.'

The tall youth bowed low, his floppy mane of hair falling over his brow. 'Yes, I've just had a little collection of verse published by Bronski Press, *Amber in the Afternoon*. I brought some copies with me. They're in my room. Perhaps you'd like one. I could sign it for you.'

'That would be jolly decent of you, Mr Callow...' said Wilde with as much enthusiasm as he could muster. Modern poetry with its discordant rhythms and gloomy messages was certainly not his thing. He was a Keats and Shelley man.

The poet gave a whinnying laugh, revealing a row of tombstone teeth. 'Oh, Jonquil, please,' he cried. 'The last person to call me Mr Callow was my Latin tutor at university.'

There was something rather comical and yet disturbing about this young man that strangely unnerved Wilde. It seemed to him that Callow was rather playing the part of the poet for effect.

The next person to be introduced to Wilde was a young lady of a studious aspect, wearing a drab, loose-fitting black dress and thick horn-rimmed spectacles perched precariously on her nose. Her hair was somewhat unruly and looked as though it had not seen a comb for some days. Nevertheless, she was strangely attractive with dark mournful eyes and arched brows. Her nose was long and sharp and her lips thin and finely curled. Wilde thought she must only be somewhere in her mid-twenties. She had been chatting to Jonquil Callow a few moments earlier but he had moved away when he and

24

Julia approached.

'Ah, Stella, my dear,' said Lady Julia in her attentive hostess mode, 'this is my nephew, Rupert Wilde.'

She eyed Rupert with a certain amount of suspicion as though he were a suspect in an identity parade. What she saw was a tall, lean, self-assured young man in a beautifully cut three-piece suit—a product of Saville Row, no doubt. He had a long face with aquiline features topped by a gentle thatch of fine blonde hair. She had to admit that he had a pair of the most startling blue eyes and a kindly expression.

'Stella Bond,' she said in a surprisingly deep, throaty, and rather sexy voice. 'I'm a valuer and conservator of paintings and *objets d'art*. I was attached to Soames of Bond Street, but now I work freelance.' She presented the information briskly as though she was attending a job interview. Despite her brusque delivery, there was a spark of passion in those eyes held prisoner by the serious spectacles.

'Sounds fascinating,' said Wilde.

'I've been carrying out an inventory of the paintings in the house here and valuing them. Algernon, Mr Markham, kindly invited me to stay over Christmas.'

'Yes, Stella has been spending quite some time here looking at our paintings. We're hoping she'll find a masterpiece,' remarked Julia with a nervous smile.

'And have you?' asked Wilde lightly.

The girl avoided the question with a non-committal raise of the eyebrow and then looked directly at Wilde with a stern expression. 'And what do you do?'

Good point, he thought. 'At the moment I am a man of leisure, looking around for the right kind of occupation to take my fancy.' He knew it was a facile comment but at present, he was not prepared or even capable of expressing his own feelings on this matter. He wasn't prepared to confess to this stranger that he did want to do something useful, to make some sort of difference, but as yet he was still coming to terms with his post-war self.

It was obvious from Stella Bond's expression that she was not impressed with his reply but that was of no consequence to him. It wasn't the first time he had been dismissed as an empty-headed lounger.

'We're doing the rounds, dear,' interposed Lady Julia. 'Making sure everyone knows everyone else before we dine tonight.'

Stella Bond gave a tight smile of acknowledgment before Julia dragged Wilde over to the corner of the room where a well-built red-faced man in a tweed suit was sitting in an armchair smoking a cheroot. Wilde placed him in his early fifties, but he reasoned that the fellow's weight and the grey hair at the temples could be disguising a slightly younger man.

'Hello, Bertie,' chirruped Lady Julia in greeting.

The man's rubicund features lit up. 'Hello, my dear. Sorry if I seem a bit of a party pooper, sitting here on my lonesome. Just needed a smoke and not everyone takes to my little pleasure.' He waved the cheroot in the air. 'Strong smell and all that. Certainly will get into the swing of things when I get some chow down me.'

'Oh, Bertie, there are no rules here. It's Christmas and you are our guest. Do please yourself. Allow me to introduce my nephew, Rupert Wilde.'

The man rose to his feet and grabbed Wilde's hand in a vigorous shake. He was short, which made his bulk seem all the more overpowering. 'Pleased to meet you, sir,' he crowed heartily, his voice's rough edge betraying his northern roots. 'Lady Julia has told me all about you, singing your praises. I gather you did very well in the blasted war. Major, wasn't it?'

'Yes, sir.'

'Call me Bertie. Hate standing on ceremony.'

'Indeed we all call him Bertie,' said Julia, 'but he really is Bertram John Silverside, head of Silverside Motors. You've no doubt heard of them, Rupert.'

Indeed he had. The firm was *the* up-and-coming motor manufacturer since the war.

'Very pleased to meet you indeed...Bertie. I particularly like the look of your new sedan, the Silver Flash.'

Bertie Silverside nodded his head vigorously. 'Aye, I'm damned proud of that little beauty myself. She goes like a dream thanks to our innovations with the suspension. Fine engine, too, of course. I can easily arrange a test drive for you, young feller, if you so wish.'

'That would be wonderful.' It was the only response he could make. Wilde really had no interest in swopping his red roadster for a new model. Sometimes polite conversation can lead you into awkward situations.

Before Bertie could respond, he was interrupted by the voice of Algernon Markham. He stood with his back to the fireplace and raised his glass. 'Ladies and gentlemen,' he said, 'welcome to Pelham House – journeys end in lovers' meeting, eh? If that's not too rum a thing to say. Here's wishing you all a Merry Christmas. There is just one more guest to arrive, Doctor Locke, our local GP, but we are nearly a full complement—a sort of complements of the season, eh?' He gave a brief embarrassed guffaw. The assembled guests smiled dutifully in response. 'It is seven now and we dine at eight-thirty so I suggest we break up this little shindig in order for you to retire to your rooms, giving you time to refresh yourselves and dress for dinner.'

There was a murmur of agreement and the guests began to drift out of the room.

'We'll talk further on cars, young man' said Bertie, dropping back down into the armchair. It was quite clear he was going nowhere until he had finished his cheroot.

Lady Julia sidled up to Wilde and took his arm. 'I do hope you'll have a nice time with us,' she said. 'It's so good to have you under my roof again, my dear sister's boy. You're in your old room, the blue chamber.'

'You'll have to remind me where it is. This house is a warren of corridors and it is some time since I was last here.'

She giggled at the idea. 'Up the stairs, turn left then first right. Come now, after reading about your little detective adventure in the papers, I'm sure you'll be able work that out.'

'And Kishen, my assistant, is next door?'

Lady Julia's smile faltered. 'Yes, as you requested. It's the small yellow room. I must say I do find it a little odd that you've taken on...a colonial as your assistant.'

'He's an excellent fellow—more a companion than an assistant. Bright as a button, Oxford-educated, reliable and charming.'

'No doubt,' she replied, without too much conviction. 'But I was surprised by your request that he join us for dinner. I mean to say a servant and...'

'He is not a servant. As I said, he is my assistant.'

'But...I mean...Is it *de rigeur*?'

'Because he's an Indian?'

'Well, yes.'

'Come now, Aunt Julia, I didn't expect such small-minded attitudes from you.'

'Well, it's not me, Rupert' she said with a dismissive wave of the hand. 'It will be the other guests.'

'If they haven't been in the company of a cultured Indian fellow before, it's time they were.'

Aunt Julia did not look convinced. 'If you say so, my dear.'

With a shrug of the shoulders, she moved away, mingling with the departing guests. After a moment's pause, Wilde also headed for the door, bumping into Stella Bond as he did so. She gave him a perfunctory smile as he apologised and then she made her way to have words with Algernon. They immediately struck up an intense somewhat heated conversation. As Wilde passed by he just caught a snatch of what they were saying which was carried out in hushed strained tones. 'I'm trying,' he said. 'Not hard enough, Mr Markham' she snapped, somewhat sarcastically, adding, 'remember you only have until Boxing Day.'

* * *

On reaching his room, Wilde tapped on the neighbouring door and received a muffled, 'Please come in.'

Kishen was stretched out on the bed reading a book, a copy of *David Copperfield* he had brought with him. He suspected there would be long hours when he could escape to his room and lose himself in Dickens' world.

'Time to get ready for dinner, old chap,' said Wilde, leaning idly against a chest of drawers.

Kishen frowned and shifted awkwardly in the bed. 'I'm not sure this is a good idea. I don't believe that I am welcome here.'

'Nonsense,' Wilde said, almost automatically, and then paused a moment. 'Why d'you say that? Has something happened?'

'Nothing really.'

'What? You must tell me.'

'It is insignificant.'

'It is not insignificant if it has made you feel unwelcome in this house. Now, come along, old boy, be honest with me.'

Kishen gave a heavy sigh. 'Well, it was when I was being shown to my room. The chap who escorted me was a touch rude.'

'A touch rude? In what way?'

Kishen sighed. 'He referred to me as a *brown boy*. He asked me where my turban was and if I was going to do the Indian rope trick as after-dinner entertainment.'

Wilde was furious. 'The Devil he did. I'll have a bally good word with the scoundrel.'

'No, no, please I beg of you. Do not stir up the waters. Let it be. I live with these sleights as a matter of course. I have had far worse said to me.'

Wilde nodded grimly; he could imagine the injustices which his friend had encountered in his short life.

'But not while you were in the house of my family as my guest.'

Kishen slid off the bed and placed his hands together as though in prayer. 'I beg you, Rupert, take this matter no further.'

There was a long pause before Wilde replied. 'Very well,' he said with some reluctance. 'For your sake, I will do as you ask, but it irritates the hell out of me. If that damned fellow puts another foot wrong, you must tell me and I will certainly sort him out.'

Kishen smiled.

'Now it's time to get the old dinner togs on. Christmas Eve dinner is at eight-thirty,' Wilde said. 'We'll go down together so you won't feel so isolated.'

* * *

While Wilde washed, shaved, and changed into his dinner suit he considered his fellow diners for this evening. There was the somewhat strangely mismatched couple, Aubrey Sinclair and his wife Sonia Lane. She still exuded an air of flamboyance and glamour and there were rumours of a series of affairs with her leading men. By contrast, the hubby seemed a rather dour, humourless old stick who, Wilde thought, exhibited no charisma whatsoever. No wonder the lady liked to play away from home. Perhaps it was a marriage of convenience: he wrote the plays in which she starred. When he had seen her in *What Matters is Murder*, she was the best thing about it; she brought radiance and excitement to the drama. The play itself was, to Wilde's mind, a rather dull creaky old warhorse. Without Sonia, it would have been nothing. Well, he thought, she herself had referred to the piece as 'that old thing.' It was as though she was passing judgment on her husband.

Then there was the epicene fellow, the poet Jonquil Callow. No doubt he was one of Aunt Julia's little projects. She liked to take a budding writer or artist under her wing to help promote their work, in an effort to launch them on a glittering career. Sadly, she usually chose individuals with mediocre talent whose voyage foundered once she had removed her support. Wilde had no real notion of the quality of Callow's verse but his instinct led him to think that it would be dull and obscure at best and probably dire.

Wilde had to admit that he was intrigued by Stella Bond. She was obviously a very pretty girl, possibly even beautiful, but she had hidden her charms with large spectacles, wild unruly hair, and a drab ill-fitting dress. Why did she do this? he pondered. Maybe she wished to discourage the attentions of men, or it could be that she believed that she wouldn't be taken seriously in her academic role if she revealed her femininity. He understood that. Young, pretty, intelligent women are rarely taken seriously by men. The nonsensical 'where there is beauty there are no brains' syndrome. He would like to discover more about Miss Bond. He was also intrigued by her statement to Algernon that he only had 'until Boxing Day.' What did she mean by that? There was certainly an underlying threat in her pronouncement.

Another puzzling character was the bluff northerner, Bertie Silverside, as he liked to be called. Wilde was sure that although he presented himself as an easy-going, hail-fellow-well-met chappie, this was a mask hiding a cool-headed, shrewd personality beneath. One did not rise to become the head of one of the most important automobile manufacturers in the country without being tough, ruthless, and cunning.

Aunt Julia had certainly assembled a fascinating cast for her Christmas jamboree, although they hardly fitted her description of 'a jolly crowd'. And added to this exotic mix was himself, the war hero who had demonstrated some detective skills but who now seemed to have settled for the role of indolent man about town who had the temerity to bring his Indian servant to the dining table.

Of course, he mused, as he checked his appearance in the full-length mirror on the wardrobe, he was forgetting his hosts in this list of dramatis personae. Well, his aunt he knew was kind and appeared a little dippy but there were hidden depths there that he had never been able to fathom. She had been married to Algernon for four years after a very short courtship. Wilde had only been in Algernon's company a few times and he had not quite worked the fellow out either. He seemed a diffident, simplistic cove, and yet there must be more to him than that. Surely? He had certainly landed on his feet marrying Julia. He brought but a few crumbs to the matrimonial coffers. If I were a cynical soul, mused Wilde, I'd think that he'd got hold of a very pleasant meal ticket.

Just as he was about to leave the room, there was a gentle tap on the door. Wilde assumed that it would be Kishen, ready to place his head in the lion's mouth. Adjusting his bow tie one more time – the devil wouldn't lie straight – he answered the door. There on the threshold was Sonia Lane.

'Hello,' he said, keeping the surprise out of his voice

'Mr Wilde, I am sorry to bother you, but I think you may be able to help me.'

She spoke the words simply, but he could see that there was real fear in her eyes.

Chapter Four

With magisterial solemnity, Boldwood helped Doctor John Locke shrug off his overcoat. There were flakes of snow on his shoulders. 'I'm even later than anticipated,' he was saying. 'I had to make an extra call on Mrs Waters in the village. She's rather a hypochondriac I'm afraid but I didn't want to desert her on Christmas Eve and have her fret all over the holiday. She just has a bit of a cold but in her eyes, it was a fatal bout of pneumonia.'

Boldwood moved his lips into what was the closest he came to a smile. 'I hope you were able to put her mind at rest.'

'I believe so.' Locke glanced at his pocket watch. 'Eight fifteen. Made it by the skin of my teeth. Luckily I had the foresight to change into my dinner suit this afternoon before setting off on my rounds. Could you carry my luggage up to my quarters and I'll make my way to the dining room.'

'Very good, sir. You are in the purple room on the second floor.'

'I can't remember the last time I wore a dinner jacket. I'm afraid it is not an example of the height of fashion. Do I look presentable,' asked Locke as he brushed away imaginary dust from the sleeve of his jacket.

'Eminently, sir.'

'Oh, just leave me my medical bag. I have some headache pills in there for Lady Julia which I need to give her later. I'll just stow it away here at the foot of the umbrella stand. I'll pass the pills over at the end of the evening, save me going all the way up to my room … on the second floor,' he added with emphasis, his voice tinged with a note of disdain. Not quite in the attic, then, he thought.

'As you wish, sir.'

Locke placed his bag by the umbrella stand and went off to the dining room.

* * *

Rupert Wilde invited Sonia Lane into his room. She held a white envelope in her hand and was fiddling with it nervously. Her whole demeanour was so different from that of earlier in the evening. The lady who had played the part of the famous actress now appeared apprehensive and uncertain.

'How do you think I can help you?' he asked gently.

'I read of your involvement with Scotland Yard in the investigation into Lady Dobney's missing tiara. "Excellent detective work," the *Clarion* said.'

Wilde smiled. 'I had no idea that my fame had spread to the pages of the *Clarion*.'

'They appeared to think you were a regular Sherlock Holmes.'

'That seems somewhat of an exaggeration. Is that why you have come to see me?'

She nodded and held out the envelope. 'I received this in the post this morning.'

The envelope contained a fairly ordinary Christmas card featuring a robin perched on the snowy bough of a fir tree. However, the message inside was far from ordinary or full of seasonal cheer: 'Merry Christmas, slut – although I doubt that you'll survive beyond Boxing Day.'

'It's horrible,' she moaned, tears welling in her eyes.

'Not the usual festive greeting, I grant you. This may seem a silly question, but I have to ask it: do you have any idea who sent the card?'

She shook her head vigorously. 'No. It's obviously from someone with a sick mind.'

'Certainly someone who wishes to frighten you.'

'Well, he's been bloody successful.'

'Have you shown it to your husband?'

'No.'

'Why on earth not?'

'It's difficult to explain. I'm afraid there are too many skeletons in my closet. Men…I have known. Lovers, I suppose you would call them, if I'm being honest.'

'You think the card may have come from one of these men?'

She paused for a moment, wondering whether she should refute such a suggestion but then realised this would be a pointless denial.

'It is possible, I suppose,' she said with some resilience. 'Yes, I've had lovers but all were brief escapades. Nothing serious on either side. They were with charming men, younger than me. Gentlemen all. I cannot believe any of them would resort to such a threat. There was never any animosity between any of them. It was a fun interlude in our lives on both our counts. We always parted on good terms. There have never been any recriminations or unpleasantness.'

'Are you sure?'

'I was. Look, Mr Wilde, this is a death threat, isn't it?'

He gave a gentle sigh. 'I am afraid so or to be more precise it is couched in those terms.'

'Then someone intends …' She broke off and began to weep into a hurriedly produced handkerchief.

'Here in this house?' Wilde suggested.

She nodded.

'Let's have a quick snifter,' he said casually, moving to the chest of drawers, extracting a bottle of single malt and pouring generous portions into two tumblers.

'Here you are,' he said, holding out the glass to Sonia Lane. 'It will stiffen the sinews and summon up the blood.' He gave her an encouraging smile.

With some hesitation, she took the glass and took a quick swig.

'So, Sonia, if I may be so bold as to address you so informally, I think what you are suggesting is that your potential murderer is in this house right now with the intent of carrying out the dirty deed over the next few days—before Boxing Day in fact.'

She slumped down on the bed and began to cry again. 'Yes.'

'And you really have no idea who it could be.'

Another head shaking spasm. 'That is why I'm here. I've come to you for help.'

Wilde's eyes twinkled mischievously. 'How do you know it's not me?'

'That would be ridiculous.'

'Of course, it would, but if I recited the names of all the guests here tonight, you would say the same. Wouldn't you?'

'Yes. No. I don't know. I can't think straight.'

'Is it not possible that whoever sent you this card has some minor grudge against you and simply wished to spoil your Christmas? Wanted you to jump at shadows and end up a nervous wreck?'

Sonia's eyes widened as this suggestion sank in. 'I...I suppose.'

'Until today, all the guests here, including myself, were strangers to you. Isn't that so?

'Yes.'

'Why would any one of them wish to kill you?' Before she could respond to that question, Wilde added, 'I suggest that you cast that card into the wastepaper basket, forget about it altogether and simply enjoy yourself. As far as I can see this is an empty threat from some nasty beast who wishes to spoil your Christmas.'

She hesitated, gazing up at him with moist eyes. 'You really think so?'

'I do. In fact I'll do it for you.' He moved to the corner of the room and dropped the card into the wicker wastepaper basket there. 'That's it. Gone. The nightmare is over.'

Sonia took a further sip of whisky and smiled. 'I think you may be right. I suppose I overreacted. I can see that now. You have been a great help, Mr Wilde—'

'Rupert, please.'

Her smile broadened. 'Rupert, you have brought daylight to a darkened room. I thank you. I suppose I've been a silly woman but I hope you understand.'

'Of course, I do. And if you feel uneasy at any time, do come to me.'

At this point there came the booming of a gong from the lower regions of the house which echoed through the house like distant thunder.

'Ah, dinner is served,' said Wilde. 'Time to put all grim thoughts away.'

Sonia rose from the bed, leaned forward, and gave him a gentle kiss on the cheek, and then, without a word, left the room.

After her departure, Wilde stood stock still for some time, his mind deep in thought. Then he moved to the wastepaper basket and retrieved the card and examined it closely once more. There was something very fishy about this business, he mused, while seeds of a possible scenario began to germinate in his brain. His thoughts were interrupted by another knock on the door. This time it was Kishen, looking resplendent in his dinner suit. Wilde observed with a little chagrin that his bow tie was beautifully balanced.

'Ready for your grub, old lad, eh?' he said.

Kishen shook his head. 'To be honest, I would much prefer a sandwich and a glass of milk in my quarters. I'd be happy to return to the adventures of master Copperfield.'

'Courage, mon brave,' Wilde said, taking his arm.

Kishen responded with a wan smile.

'I want you to be my second pair of eyes this evening,' said Wilde as they made their way downstairs. Briefly, he told Kishen about Sonia Lane's visit to his room.

'Gracious, it sounds serious,' said Kishen solemnly.

'Indeed, I believe it is but perhaps not in the way you seem to think. What I want you to do is to keep an eye on the lady at all times and anyone who comes in close contact with her. I will point her out to you.'

'Is this a bit of detective work?'

Wilde smiled. 'Could be.'

Chapter Five

The dining room was already abuzz with conversation when they entered. Most of the guests were present, hovering around the grand dining table which sparkled in the candlelight, the cutlery gleaming and the fine china plates seeming to shimmer like a row of ghostly moons in the flickering illumination.

As Wilde and Kishen entered, all heads turned in their direction and the conversation faltered as they took in the appearance of Kishen.

Lady Julia rushed forward to greet them and shook Kishen by the hand before turning to the assembled guests. 'Ladies and gentlemen, this is Kishen; he is my nephew's ...' For a moment she seemed uncertain how to describe him. She had forgotten what Wilde had called him but she knew she should not allow the word 'servant' to pass her lips. A servant sitting at the dinner table in Pelham House was unthinkable. Eventually, she came upon the word she felt most comfortable with and which was least controversial: '... secretary.'

Kishen bowed. 'Good evening,' he said.

He received an awkward, muted response from the others.

Fortuitously for Lady Julia, at that moment Boldwood entered the room with the announcement that dinner was about to be served.

There were name cards on the table to indicate a seating plan. Wilde found that he was sandwiched between Jonquil Callow and Stella Bond. Again, she wore a very unattractive voluminous gown which to Wilde's mind resembled a shiny tent. Why was the girl determined to appear frumpy and dull? Callow placed a small volume on the table in front of Wilde. 'My

37

little opus – perhaps not magnum yet, but I have hopes,' he said, his features wreathed in an oleaginous smirk. 'I took the liberty of signing it. I do hope you will enjoy it, that the verse will speak to you.'

Wilde picked up the book and flicked through the pages, catching a glimpse of the titles of some of the poems: 'The Death of Hope', 'Burial Casket', 'Oblivion Soon', and 'Garden of Ashes.' A laugh a minute, thought Wilde. 'Thank you. I look forward to reading it,' he said, carefully placing the book under his chair.

Callow leaned across Wilde and passed another of his books to Stella Bond. 'And I couldn't resist giving a copy to you … Miss Bond.'

She seemed a little surprised but took it graciously. 'Thank you,' she said.

'And I have inscribed it,' he said pointedly.

Wilde thought she seemed a little non-plussed at this and she just nodded awkwardly.

Boldwood and two serving girls attended to the table. Wine was poured and soup was served. Wilde looked down the table where Kishen was sitting. He was involved in a stilted conversation with Bertie Silverside. Poor Kish, thought Wilde, what have I let him in for.

Stella Bond leaned over to touch his arm. 'When we talked this afternoon, I did not know you had been a Major in the war. If I seemed a little off-hand, I apologise.'

'Not necessary, I assure you. That was then. One has to adjust to the new post-war world.'

'And are you really adjusting to it by doing nothing?'

'Well, I'm waiting.'

'For what?'

'If only I knew.'

'I can't believe an intelligent and brave man like you would fritter his life away when the country needs talented individuals to take up the reins of all kinds of important jobs, doctors, engineers, scientists, lawyers …'

Wilde gave a shrug. 'My qualifications for such occupations are nil.'

'What did you do before the war?'

'After university, I travelled a bit and then joined the army for want of a better thing to do and a couple of years later the old balloon went up.'

'It seems such a shame that you are wasting your life now.' Her face was solemn and concerned. She really did care, Wilde thought, and she was not at all as he'd thought after their first meeting: a rather selfish, stand-offish cold fish.

'As I say, I'm just waiting for something to turn up. But enough about me. How long have you been a picture valuer?'

'Five years.'

'You like it.'

She nodded and her eyes flashed. 'I am passionate about it.'

'Have you spotted any gems at Pelham House?'

Stella pushed her spectacles up her nose. 'You asked me that before. I'm afraid it would be most unprofessional to discuss my client's collection.' The voice began to chill again. Wilde was aware that she was reverting to her frozen ice maiden mode. Obviously one could only go so far with this lady before the portcullis came down.

He was just about to respond when there was a scream. It rose above the idle chatter and clink of soup spoons. Looking down the table, Wilde saw Sonia Lane jumping to her feet with a strangled gasp. Her chair fell over with a heavy thump and she staggered backwards, clutching her throat with a strange gargling sound.

'What is it, darling?' cried her husband, rushing to her side.

'I've been poisoned. The wine is poisoned,' she cried. And then she turned on Sinclair, her arm thrust out towards him in a fierce accusative fashion, her eyes ablaze. 'It was you! You did it! You have poisoned me.'

For a few seconds, there was absolute silence in the room as everyone stared in shocked amazement at the woman and her dramatic accusation. Indeed, thought Wilde, it was like a scene from one of Sinclair's melodramas, only this was really happening.

'My dear …' said Aubrey Sinclair, making a move towards his wife. As he did so, she fell to the floor.

'Doctor Locke, for God's sake look to the lady,' cried Algernon Markham. The doctor, dabbing his chin with a napkin, responded to the brusque request and raced to Sonia's side. He knelt down by her side and cradled her head. Her lips quivered and her eyes fluttered wildly.

'Get me some water,' Locke said.

Most of the diners were dumbstruck by the events, apart from Bertie Silverside who was waving his arms about shouting, 'What the bloody hell is going on?'

Wilde saw that Kishen was attempting to calm him and explain, as much as he could about what had just occurred.

'Perhaps we could move the lady to the sofa in the drawing room,' said Locke.

Algernon came forward. 'Good idea. I'll give you a hand.'

Between the two of them, they carried Sonia out of the room, with Aubrey Sinclair following behind, his face creased with worry. The remaining diners looked on in silence as though witnessing a funeral cortege.

Wilde stepped forward and picked up Sonia's wine glass. The contents had hardly been touched. He took a sniff at the wine and wrinkled his nose. Deftly, unseen by the others, he exchanged Sonia's glass with his own. He was about to return to his seat when he noticed her handbag on the floor under the table. Dropping down out of sight below table level he turned his attention to the reticule. Some moments later, he felt a hand touch his shoulder. He turned and saw that it was Kishen leaning over him.

'What is all this?' he asked quietly.

Wilde looked him directly in the face. 'As I suspected. Detective work,' he said.

* * *

After a short interval, Doctor Locke reappeared. 'The lady is in no danger. I am certain she will make a full recovery. She has retired to her room. I've given her a sedative and she is sleeping now.'

'What's all that about her being poisoned? And by her husband?' asked Bertie Silverside.

Locke looked uneasy. 'That is what she says. She claims that her drink was spiked with poison and that her husband was responsible.'

'Why this is most terrible,' said Lady Julia. 'What on earth do we do?'

'She insists that the police are called and that her drink be analysed.'

'Isn't it possible the lady is just a little hysterical?' suggested Stella Bond.

'Oh, dear, this is so difficult,' said Lady Julia. She turned to Wilde. 'What do you think, Rupert? You've had some dealings with the police.'

Wilde gave a gentle shrug and without a word, he moved to where Sonia Lane had been sitting and picked up his own wine glass that he had placed there. He made a show of sniffing it and then he dipped his finger into the wine, and then placed it in his mouth. Giving a slight shake of the head, he took a drink from the glass. There was a shocked reaction from the onlookers. Lady Julia gave a whimper of fear. 'Don't be a damned fool,' bellowed Bertie Silverside.

Wilde smiled. 'Too late,' he said. 'This wine is harmless.' In a theatrical gesture, he drained the glass. 'Harmless and delicious.'

'Thank heavens,' cried Lady Julia, clapping her hands together applauding Wilde's gesture.

'Looks like the lady was just being hysterical, eh?' said Silverside.

'It would appear so, Bertie,' observed Wilde nonchalantly.

'Actresses, eh. They'll do anything to be the centre of attention.'

'I think we should resume our seats now after this little diversion and I'll inform Boldwood that the meal will continue in five minutes,' announced Algernon Markham awkwardly.

'I think I've lost my appetite,' said Stella Bond, 'but I don't want to be difficult.'

'No, dear, you don't,' observed Algernon with what Wilde thought was a dark undertone.

Like sleepy marionettes, slowly the diners began returning to their seats. As Kishen was about to follow suit, Wilde stopped him, tugging at his sleeve.

'Cover me. Stand in front of me to mask me from sight.'

Without a word, Kishen did as he was bidden, while Wilde retrieved his silver cigarette case from his pocket, dropping the contents, five cigarettes, onto the floor and pushing them under the table with his foot. Then he lifted

Sonia Lane's wine glass that he had swopped with his own and poured some of the liquid into the case before snapping it shut. 'Hope the bally thing is watertight...or rather winetight,' he muttered, as he slipped it back into his pocket, where it nestled with another recently acquired item.

'Thanks, Kish old chap. Mission accomplished. You can go back to your seat now.'

'Must I?'

Wilde chuckled. 'Fraid so.'

'I am hoping mysteries will be explained in due course,' Kishen whispered.

'Indeed they will—as you say, in due course.'

The meal resumed shortly afterwards without further incident although the conversation was somewhat stilted and there were long periods of silence apart from the clinking of cutlery.

After dessert, Algernon Markham announced that they were dispensing with the traditional dinner party ritual which involved the ladies leaving the room while the gentlemen smoked. He invited all the guests into the large drawing room where drinks and coffee were being served, adding, 'And with the ladies' kind permission – there are only two of you now – the men are allowed to smoke should they wish to.'

'Good idea, Algy,' roared Bertie Silverside. 'Never did like the notion of losing the charm of the fairer sex in exchange for a smoke. You lead the way, old boy.'

As the diners vacated their seats slowly and progressed into the drawing room, Wilde caught up with his aunt.

'I'm sorry about the distraction earlier,' he said, giving her a hug.

'Yes, it has rather taken the bloom off the occasion. There's little Christmas spirit about now. I don't know what I'm going to do.'

'People will come round, you'll see. What's happened to Sonia and Aubrey?'

Julia rolled her eyes. 'I should never have invited them. I knew they were having trouble – marital problems, although they never made it public. Certainly, they've never caused such a scene like the one here tonight. Poison! I ask you.' She paused, her frown growing deeper. 'You don't think he really tried to poison her, do you?'

Wilde shook his head. 'I just think the actress in her took over.'

'You mean she was imagining it…?'

'Or lying.'

Julia's eyebrows shot up. 'Do you really believe that?'

Wilde replied with a gentle non-committal smile.

'If that is the case, she is a wicked woman trying to get her husband in trouble with the police.'

'I assume that you have found Aubrey another room for the night. No doubt they'll not be sharing quarters after tonight's debacle.'

'Yes, Boldwood arranged all that in his usual efficient manner. I suspect they'll leave in the morning. I do hope so; I don't want any more tantrums at Pelham House.'

While this conversation was taking place, Stella Bond had attached herself to Kishen.

'You are a Hindu, I believe?' She said it sweetly but he was aware that there was a note of interrogation in her voice.

'That is correct. How did you guess?'

'Apart from the fact that you didn't drink any of the wine at dinner, there is a little pin in your lapel which I believe represents the Om, the Hindu symbol for ultimate reality.'

Kishen bowed his head. 'You are quite right. Well spotted.'

'I am a picture valuer and conservator. It is my job to spot small details. India fascinates me. Asian art is remarkable. The richness of the colours, the esoteric designs. I'd love to go there and soak up its atmosphere and influence. However, as things are in my life I doubt if that is going to be possible. Not for the immediate future anyway.'

'Indeed the art is remarkable, but India is a poor country. There is much poverty. Extravagance rubs shoulders with extreme penury.'

'You have no desire to return?'

'Someday, but I so admire the British way of life, its customs, and freedoms. I am very happy here.'

'We are not without the poor in this country. Do not be misled by your current surroundings and the grand folk flouting their wealth and privilege here. You should see the slums in the east end of London, for instance, and struggles that great numbers of agricultural folk in the countryside have to endure.'

'I am well aware of all that. My final paper at university was about Britain's change from agriculturalism to industrialism in the nineteenth century.'

'Yes, the bloody machines squeezing the spirit out of the human soul.' Her voice had risen in pitch and her cheeks had flushed with emotion.

'You sound most passionate about such things.'

'I am a very passionate person,' she replied stoically. Suddenly she turned her head, looking over Kishen's shoulder. 'Excuse me, I need to have words with Algernon.' She was gone in an instant.

Kishen was about to make his way over to Wilde to state that he had done his duty by attending this strange party and to request that he be released from his obligations and retire to his bedroom. As he did so, he observed Bertram Silverside bearing down on him.

'Oh, my goodness,' he muttered under his breath. The last thing he wanted just now was another lecture on how the importation of the motor car into India would bring increased prosperity to the land. He made a swift about-turn and casually as possible he circumnavigated the room in order to approach Wilde from a different direction.

'If it is agreeable to you, I would like to return to my room now,' said Kishen, catching up with Wilde at last, but before he was able to respond, Silverside bore down on them.

'Rum do tonight, eh, Wilde? Not the kind of Christmas party I was expecting.'

Wilde gave a non-committal nod.

'Strange set of people to be honest. Present company excepted of course. What d'you make of that lass with the glasses?' He turned to Kishen. 'She seemed to be getting hot under the collar with you just now.' He leaned nearer. 'What was she telling you?'

Kishen was non-plussed by this query. He regarded it as rather rude and it took him a few seconds to summon a reply. 'It was casual talk really. We ... discussed Indian art.'

'Is that all? Are you sure?'

'Yes, of course.'

Silverside did not look convinced.

'Please excuse us, Bertie,' said Wilde, taking hold of Kishen's arm. 'I have some private business to discuss with my secretary.' Without another word, Wilde led Kishen to the door and out in the hall.

'This is a most mysterious evening, Rupert. Not what I expected at all.'

Wilde grinned. 'Me neither. And all the better for that. I have something to tell you and to show you. Let's go into the library.'

Before they could reach the door, Wilde was approached by Jonquil Callow. He was holding out a copy of his poetry book. 'You forgot this, Rupert. You left it under your chair,' he said pointedly.

'How remiss of me,' Wilde replied smoothly.

At this point, Stella Bond approached. 'Mr Callow,' she said brightly. 'I think this is yours.' She held up her hand, her palm outstretched revealing a bright blue cufflink.

Callow gazed at it for a moment and then checked his cuffs.

'Yes. It must have slipped out. Thank you.'

'It is lovely. I thought it would be precious to you.'

'It ... it is,' he said.

She smiled briefly and then moved away.

'Time we were on our way, too,' said Wilde. 'Thank you again for the book.'

Callow turned and without a word wandered towards the drinks table.

'Strange behaviour,' observed Kishen. 'How did she know that was Mr Callow's cufflink?'

'That was the very question that was on my mind also. Intriguing, indeed. But now, let's make our way to the library.'

As the pair crossed the hall, Doctor Locke was descending the staircase. He looked weary and careworn.

'Ah, the very man,' cried Wilde, approaching him.

Locke raised a quizzical eyebrow.

'How is the patient, Doctor?'

'I've just checked on her. Still sleeping, but she is in no danger.'

'Oh, of that I'm certain.'

Locke seemed a little surprised at Wilde's assured response but did not question it. 'I believe her problem is psychological rather than physical. But that is a realm beyond my expertise,' said Locke running his fingers through his hair wearily.

'I am sure you are correct,' agreed Wilde. 'Now, I was just about to tell a little story to my assistant Kishen here and provide a small demonstration which I believe will provide an explanation of tonight's little drama. Would you care to accompany us to the library and join in the fun?'

Chapter Six

Once ensconced in the library, Rupert Wilde seated his companions in leather easy chairs and took centre stage.

'Before dinner this evening, I was visited in my room by Sonia Lane,' he began, leaning casually against a reading table in the centre of the room. 'She showed me a mysterious Christmas card she claimed to have received. The message inside was a death threat, saying that she would not survive Christmas.'

'Great Scott!' exclaimed Locke.

'I convinced her that it was most likely a hoax. Who amongst the guests would wish to kill her? They were all strangers to her – except one. It was obvious to me that she was in a roundabout fashion pointing the accusing finger at her husband, Aubrey Sinclair. She was using me, alerting me to the possibility that he would attempt to kill her. It was a ploy instigated for her own nefarious purposes.'

'Why did she come to you?' asked Locke.

Wilde gave a gentle shrug. 'She had read about my involvement with a police investigation and no doubt thought that I possessed some detective skills and that I would put two and two together and back her accusations. Who would most likely wish to kill her amongst a set of strangers? The only person she knew intimately and could have a credible motive: her husband. She admitted to me that she had been unfaithful to him on several occasions. Poisoning her would be his revenge. On examining the Christmas card closely after she had left the room, I determined that the message had most likely been written by a woman. The handwriting was neat and yet there were extravagant flourishes in the formation of some of the letters which indicated a feminine hand. No doubt an expert comparing it with Sonia's own handwriting would be able to establish the similarity.'

'But the poisoning. Why would she poison herself?'

Wilde shook his head. 'She didn't. The poisoning episode was too dramatic, too theatrical, in fact, to bear the mark of credibility. Remember the lady is an actress. If her husband really meant to kill her, surely he would have chosen a more subtle method and a less public arena.'

'And, in fact, you proved her wine was not tainted with poison by drinking it,' said Locke.

'Ah, but her wine was tainted. I managed to switch glasses before I gallantly downed the contents of my own giving the impression that it was hers.' Wilde produced his cigarette case from his pocket, laid it on the table, and opened it carefully. Locke and Kishen peered closely at it. There was a puddle of red liquid inside.

'This is a sample of Sonia Lane's wine that I managed to retrieve. 'Take a sniff at it, Doctor.'

Locke did so and let out a gasp of surprise. 'Bitter almonds. Cyanide, by Jove.'

'No, just bitter almonds, enough to create the impression that the wine was spiked with cyanide. It would have been a fairly convincing job, despite the fact that she had only taken a sip of wine but, as I am sure you know, cyanide does not affect the victim instantly.'

'Indeed, it takes time to reach the stomach and cause a reaction. Why this is amazing,' said Locke.

Kishen chuckled. 'It is like something out of a detective story.'

'Then there is this ...' Wilde dipped his hand into his jacket pocket and produced a small glass phial which had a cork in the top. The phial was a quarter full of a milky liquid.

'What is that?' asked Locke.

Wilde uncorked the phial and held it under the doctor's nose. 'A concoction of bitter almonds,' he said.

Kishen also took a sniff. 'Gracious, it is very pungent.'

'I retrieved the phial from Sonia Lane's handbag after she performed her extravagant fainting fit. I believe that she slipped some of this liquid into her drink to create the impression that her wine was indeed laced with cyanide. No doubt it's a trick that had been used in one of the murder mystery plays she's appeared in.' He chuckled. 'Probably one written by her husband.'

'That is amazing. The cunning devil,' observed the doctor.

'As I intimated earlier, I learned tonight that the marriage was in difficulty.' Wilde smiled. 'That phrase now seems something of an understatement. It appears that Sonia was determined not only to get rid of her husband but also have him arrested for attempted murder.'

'She is either a cruel-hearted beast or a desperate woman,' observed Kishen.

Locke leaned forward in his chair. 'Gentlemen, I can tell you when I ministered to the lady just now, I noted the remnants of severe bruising on her arms. Obviously, she has suffered some hurt at the hands of another.'

'Her husband, no doubt,' said Wilde. 'He certainly seemed to me to be the awkward bullying type.'

Kishen stroked his chin. 'If that is the case then they almost seem to be as bad as each other.'

'What happens now?' asked Locke.

'Well, no crime has actually been committed so there is no reason for us to be involved any further in the matter. It is rather a complicated and sordid business. However, I suggest that in the morning I speak to them both, revealing all that I know and advise them that they act responsibly and file for divorce and go their separate ways as soon as possible. They are a danger to each other. Then it is up to them how they behave, but I suspect that with the truth of their relationship out in the open there will be no more failed murder attempts or domestic violence.'

'That sounds a very reasonable suggestion, Wilde. I assume that we are to keep these details amongst ourselves.'

Wilde nodded. 'I think that would be for the best.'

Locke stretched and sighed. 'I must say it has been a very interesting evening. After a day ministering to patients with minor ailments of coughs, colds, and rheumatism, the last thing I expected was to be involved in a pseudo murder drama over dinner.' He gave a little laugh. 'I suppose it has added some spice to the Christmas season. Now, I think it's time I climbed those wooden hills to Bedfordshire. Good evening, gentlemen.' With a gentle wave of his hand, he left the room.

'And I reckon you're ready for bed now, eh, Kish old chap.'

'Most decidedly.'

'Off you go then. I'll just say my goodnight to our hosts before I follow suit.'

* * *

On re-entering the drawing room, Wilde found that most of the other guests had also retired for the night. The Sonia Lane farrago had thrown a very wet blanket over the proceedings. There was only Aunt Julia, Algernon, and Bertie Silverside still present. Julia was sitting in an armchair cradling what Wilde assumed was a large gin and tonic. She looked drained and her vacant staring eyes indicated that she was lost in thought. Unpleasant reminiscences of tonight's debacle clouding her mind, no doubt. The two men were standing by the curtained window in deep hushed conversation. Algernon was waving his arms about in a demonstrative fashion while Silverside was shaking his head in a gesture that suggested he was rejecting whatever Algernon was saying. It took all three of them some time to register that Wilde had entered the room. Aunt Julia was the first one to speak. 'Oh, Rupert, dear, I thought you'd gone to bed.'

'That's where I'm going now,' he said, crossing to her and planting a kiss on her forehead. 'I just came in to say good night – and see how you were.'

'Well, my dear, I feel somewhat wretched if you must know. Tonight has been a trial, to say the least.'

'Things won't look so bad in the morning.'

'You may be right. I'll feel a lot happier when those two are out of this house.' Her face did not reflect her sentiments. To Wilde, there seemed to be something more than the theatrical antics of Sonia Lane preying on Julia's mind. He felt prompted to probe a little, but Julia's sad stoical features told him that he would not get very far with his enquiries this evening. He resigned himself to placing the matter on hold.

'Good night, darling. Sleep well,' he said, squeezing her arm gently.

She responded with a wan smile. 'I rarely do. Insomnia, you know. That's why I have my own bedroom so I don't disturb Nonny.'

'Nonny?'

She gave a bleak smile. 'Algernon. It's a pet name.'

Wilde gave her another kiss on her forehead and then turned to the two men by the window. 'And goodnight to you, gentlemen.' He gave them a casual salute.

They waved and muttered suitable responses.

As Rupert Wilde made his weary way up the stairs towards his room, his mind was full of dark thoughts and tantalising questions. He wasn't a superstitious man but something was telling him that there was still very much amiss in Pelham House. He dreaded to think what the morrow would bring.

Chapter Seven

Aubrey Sinclair could not sleep. It was three o'clock in the morning and he had not had a moment's shuteye since laying his head on the cold and starchy pillow in his new room, the one he had been removed to after his wife's hysterical, accusative performance at dinner. To begin with, he was not used to sleeping alone or contemplating the ruin of his marriage and his reputation. What had possessed the silly vindictive bitch to create such a scene and make such a ridiculous claim? The old girl must be going gaga or she hated him so much…. What the hell was going to happen now? Separation, divorce, vilification in the press. Of, course, Sonia would see to that. 'Read all about it: Famous Playwright attempts Murder. Distraught Wife Tells All.' Despite the fact that it was a load of nonsense, a cruel trick performed by that crazy woman with no evidence to back her malicious claims, he would become a pariah in the theatre world. The public would lap up the travesty. Who would employ a playwright who had tried to poison his wife—although he bloody well hadn't—and, of course, that wife being the beloved Sonia Lane, she would receive nothing but sympathy and adulation. The cow had planned the whole thing perfectly. Oh, Christ! As these thoughts thundered around his brain, he concluded that it was no wonder he couldn't sleep. 'And a flaming Merry Christmas to you, Aubrey,' he muttered bitterly to himself in self-pitying tones as he lay on his back, arms rigidly by his side, staring up at the ornate ceiling, almost wishing the damned thing would crash down upon his head and end his life. That would solve everything!

And then another irritation impinged on his sleeplessness. There were noises from the room next door. Whoever was in there was being very irresponsible making such a row at this time of night. There were muffled sounds and then what sounded like an item of furniture falling over – a chair maybe. Then, his body stiffened with apprehension as he thought he heard a muffled scream.

Was it his imagination?

Surely?

He sat up in bed straining his ears, but now strangely there was silence. All had gone quiet. He waited a few seconds but still heard nothing. Had he imagined the scream? No, he had not. He was certain about that. Slipping out of bed, he donned his dressing gown and went to the door. Pressing his ear close to the wood, he listened. He heard the creak of hinges as though someone was leaving or entering the adjoining room.

Taking a deep breath, he stepped tentatively out into the dimly lighted corridor and saw someone emerging from his neighbour's bedroom. What caught his attention and chilled him to the marrow was the sight of the vicious knife the shadowy figure was grasping in its hand, the blade apparently dripping with a dark substance – which, he reasoned, had to be blood. On seeing this, he gave an audible gasp and froze. This alerted the dark figure to his presence. It turned round slowly and saw him.

'You,' he cried in recognition as the face came into view.

Raising the knife, the intruder advanced towards him. He could not move, transfixed with shock and fear as the figure bore down on him. Before he could cry out, he saw the flash of the blade as it was raised high, and then he felt the knife slice into his flesh. He was stabbed once in the chest, and then twice in the stomach. Pain electrified his body and he writhed and squirmed with the ferocity of his wounds. The trauma was so great that despite his mouth working wildly no sound was able to emerge. It was like in a nightmare in which he screamed silently. He staggered a few feet before collapsing to the floor in agony. As his face hit the carpet, he saw his assailant disappearing down the corridor towards the staircase.

His vision dimmed as life seeped from his body, but after a few seconds, Aubrey Sinclair managed to raise himself onto his hands and knees and, resembling some huge grotesque mechanical toy, he summoned up sufficient energy to crawl his way slowly along the corridor to the head of the stairs, leaving a thin trail of blood in his wake. Once there, he paused, his ability to think fading fast. Suddenly, with a Herculean effort, by grabbing hold of the banister rail, he managed to raise himself to his feet. He stood for some seconds at the top of the stairs, his body wavering unsteadily, and then, bracing himself, he let out a frantic cry for help. His thick, croaky plea echoed faintly through the dark and silent house. It was like a terrible nightmare. His faint cries evaporated in the blackness; there was no one to hear him. He tried to call out once more but the painful effort drained him of what feeble energy he had left, his efforts causing him to stumble and stagger forward. In an instant, he lost his footing and with a silent howl of horror, he crashed down the stairs, his body like a rag doll, arms, and legs flailing wildly, as he rolled and bumped erratically to the bottom.

He lay there in the hall, his head twisted sideways, the wild dead eyes staring sightlessly at the twinkling Christmas tree.

Chapter Eight

I t was Boldwood who found the body in the early morning. As was his practice, he was the first up and about the house in readiness for his duties of the day, making sure everything ran efficiently from dawn till dusk. After making the gruesome discovery, his initial action was to throw a blanket over the deceased, and then he went to waken Algernon and Lady Julia to pass on the grim news.

Lady Julia had a few moments of hysteria before Algernon came into her room and managed to calm her down.

'Don't fret, my dear,' he said, 'Boldwood and I will sort things out. You rest awhile.'

Julia slumped back in the bed, still a little tearful, but her emotions now more or less held in check.

Algernon went with Boldwood to view the body. 'Gracious, how horrible,' he said, kneeling down to examine the wounds. 'We can't leave the poor devil here at the bottom of the stairs. It's the first thing the guests will see when they come down. We'll have hysteria run riot. Oh, God, and I'll have to tell Sonia the news. What an unholy mess.'

In the end, they carried the body of Aubrey Sinclair to the library and locked the door. 'You clean up the blood at the bottom of the stairs, Boldwood, and I'll go and have a word with Mr Wilde. The police will have to be informed and he may well know what we should do.'

Rupert Wilde was lying on his back in bed, gently stretching his limbs and wishing he had a cup of hot, strong tea to energise his body for the new day. He had allowed his mind to wander, thinking once more about the guests that Julia and Algernon has assembled for their Christmas house party. They were, to say the least, a strange and disparate bunch. Not one of them was really a true friend of the couple, a fact that said much about the social isolation of his aunt and her comparatively new hubby. Were there no real dyed in the wool chums they could clasp to their bosom at this special season to share the festive cheer? Apparently not. It was very sad.

He was roused from this reverie by a loud knock at his door. Perhaps this was a maid with a tray containing such a beverage as he desired. 'Come in,' he called. He was most surprised to see that his visitor was Algernon Markham. His face was dark and his eyes held a strange faraway look as though he was in some kind of trance.

'There's been a murder,' he announced without ceremony.

* * *

'Well, he appears to have been stabbed rather viciously three times, and the angle of his head suggests that his neck was broken as a result of the fall,' said Wilde after he had examined the body. He turned to Doctor Locke who had also been summoned to view the corpse.

'Indeed, that is a fair assessment, Mr Wilde,' agreed the medic.

'He was probably attacked at the top of the stairs and fell down them. We must look to see if there are any signs of blood on the landing. It's a pity that the body had to be moved. The police won't like that.'

'Maybe not,' said Markham brusquely 'but I just couldn't leave the thing lying there, having the others stepping over it.'

'Of course, I understand. Well, Christmas Day or no, we'll have to call the police in. It's all very unpleasant. You realise, of course, that whoever did this is one of the guests in this house.'

'Great Scott. I hadn't thought about that.' Markham paused, his jaw dropping. 'Sonia! You don't think? Surely not.'

'It's too early to be pointing accusative fingers. It is true there was some strong animosity between her and Sinclair but whether she would be reckless and indeed inflamed enough to carry out such a brutal act is something we cannot be sure about at the moment.'

'I suppose I'd better summon the others and let them know what has happened.' Markham ran his fingers through his mane of grey hair and groaned. 'So terrible, so terrible.'

'Sonia should be informed on her own, in her room. Who knows what her reaction will be. Whatever, she ought to be told in private,' Wilde observed.

Markham nodded gravely. 'I don't suppose that you'd do it, would you, Rupert? I really don't feel up to it and Julia's not in a fit state either.'

Wilde nodded. 'Very well. You get some tea on the go, assemble all the guests together and pass on the grim news while I go and talk to Sonia.'

* * *

Sonia Lane stared uncomprehendingly after Wilde had told her in the gentlest of terms possible that her husband was dead – that he had been murdered. He spared her the gruesome details of the manner of his demise. Her features paled and her eyes were vacant, seeming to focus on some point over his shoulder. He reasoned that part of her behaviour would be caused by the sleeping draught that Doctor Locke had administered the night before. Indeed, it struck him that if the drug was still affecting her this morning, she would hardly have been in a fit state to rise from her bed in the early hours of the morning and seek out her husband to stab him to death.

'He is definitely dead? There is no doubt?' she said at length, her voice a dreary monotone.

'I am afraid so.'

'Poor man. The poor, poor man. How awful. I suppose that makes me a widow now.' It was at this point that the tears came. 'I loved him once, you know. It was just…' Her arms flailed like someone drowning as though she was searching for the right expression. '…that things got sour. I really was ready to leave him,' she went on brushing the tears away, 'to have him out of my life—but not like this. Oh, God, not like this.' She turned and fell back on the bed sobbing into her pillow. Wilde knew it was best not to say or do anything, just be a presence in the room. After a while, the crying stopped

57

and she dried her eyes on the bedsheet. 'Who would want to kill him? What was the motive?'

'At this moment in time, I don't know, but after a thorough investigation, I am sure the truth will emerge.'

'Investigation. That means the police.'

'Of course. A terrible crime has been committed.'

She stared blankly at him again for some seconds before replying. 'They will want to question me.'

You and everyone else in the house, including me. We are all suspects.'

Sonia Lane suddenly gave a strange, twisted grin and repeated his words like a whispered echo: 'We are all suspects.'

* * *

As Wilde was making his way downstairs he encountered Kishen. 'Ah, there you are, Rupert. I knocked at your room but there was no reply.'

'Indeed. I was awakened betimes. There have been some ugly developments overnight.'

Kishen's eyes widened. 'Oh?'

Quickly and concisely Wilde told him of Aubrey Sinclair's murder and its repercussions.

'Gracious. These are deep waters.'

'And muddy. Very muddy.'

'Any theories?'

Wilde gave a bleak smile and shook his head. 'Bit early for all that.'

'No doubt you will be donning your sleuthing hat again.'

'No doubt.'

'Well, I must say that this is the strangest English Christmas I've ever had.'

'You and me both, Kishen, old lad—but I've got to admit it's rather an interesting one.'

They entered the dining room to find most of the guests assembled, having responded to the booming of the gong. Julia, looking like a bewildered ghost, clung to her husband's arm.

'What's this all about, Algy, and where's breakfast? I've got the devil of a rumbling tum.' Bertie Silverside was gazing at the empty sideboard where he had expected dishes of kedgeree, bacon, sausages, and eggs to be laid out ready for him to gorge on.

'There's been an unfortunate development,' said Markham gravely.

By Jove, the art of understatement, thought Wilde.

'I don't want to explain until we are all here.'

'Well, there's still Miss Bond missing,' observed Jonquil casually, lighting up a cigarette.

'And Aubrey and Sonia. Unless they've done a bunk after last night's nonsense,' remarked Bertie.

Almost on cue, Sonia Lane walked into the room. Wilde was amused to see that she had made a remarkable transformation. No longer was she the picture of the pale sobbing widow she had presented in her bedroom not fifteen minutes ago. She had now flowered into a serene creature, self-possessed and immaculate in appearance, her makeup meticulously applied. She gave a faint smile of greeting.

She has dressed for the role of the self-contained tragic widow, thought Wilde. Enter, Leading Lady, stage right.

Julia rushed to her side and embraced her. Sonia took it coldly.

'I say, what's going on?' asked Jonquil. 'Can't we be told?'

'Please be patient, Jonquil,' said Lady Julia. 'Boldwood, would you go up to Miss Bond's room again and tap on her door and say that she is wanted in the dining room with some urgency.' With a regal bow, Boldwood left the room.

'We *are* going to get some breakfast, aren't we?' enquired Bertie Silverside peevishly.

'In due course, no doubt,' said Markham with a touch of irritation.

This answer did not suit Silverside and he frowned heavily.

There was an unpleasant lull in conversation until Boldwood returned a few minutes later, his normally placid features darkened with concern. He whispered some words in Markham's ear who then beckoned to Wilde to follow him.

'What now?' growled Bertie Silverside as the two men left the room.

Markham took Wilde's arm, leading him towards the staircase. 'Apparently, Boldwood cannot get any response from Miss Bond despite knocking very hard on her door. It is all very strange.' He spoke softly, failing to disguise the worried tone in his voice.

'Perhaps she is ill.'

'Yes.'

On reaching the door of Stella Bond's room, Markham knocked hard and called out her name. There was no reply. Grasping the doorknob, he turned it abruptly and opened the door, slowly, calling out her name again. There was still no response.

The room was in darkness. The curtains were drawn. Wilde switched on the light. They saw a figure in the bed. It was Stella Bond, her head peeking above the covers which were drawn up to her chin. She was not moving. She lay on her back, her long hair splayed over the pillow. Wilde moved to her side and placed the back of his hand to her cheek. It was cold. His heart sank as he realised the truth.

'She's dead, I'm afraid,' he said.

Markham gave a strange gurgling sound, his arms flapping in horror. 'Good God,' he cried when he had found the ability to speak. 'Are you sure?'

'Yes.'

'This is madness. I don't understand. How...how did she die?'

Wilde gazed down at the side of the bed and noticed the bloodstains. Gently he pulled back the sheets to reveal the girl's blood-spattered corpse. She was wearing a long cotton nightdress which was smeared with dried blood and there were several tears in the material where a knife had found entry around the chest.

On seeing this sight, Markham slumped on the edge of the bed. 'Oh, my God,' he moaned, his chest heaving with emotion. 'Stella. This is a nightmare surely? I will wake up soon.'

'Indeed, reality can be worse than a nightmare,' observed Wilde as his brain once more conjured up images of a trail of bloody corpses in a crumbling dugout somewhere in Flanders. He swallowed to suppress the rising bile and turned his attention to the practical task of inspecting the room.

Markham turned slowly and gazed down at the dead girl and the vicious wounds. 'It looks like the poor girl has been stabbed to death just like Aubrey. There must be a maniac in the house.'

'Or someone very cunning,' said Wilde softly.

'What on earth do you mean?'

'I'm not quite sure,' Wilde responded quickly, shrugging off the question. Now was not the time to discuss his thoughts or indeed reveal them. 'Look, we'd better leave her here and get on to the police straight away. I think it would be wise to keep her death a secret until they arrive. Don't let anyone else know. Is that understood?'

Markham nodded. 'If you think it wise.'

'I believe so. We'll have to say that the poor girl is ill. We'd better get Doctor Locke up here on the pretext of examining her and while he's doing that you can break the news about Aubrey and then contact the police at their headquarters in Norwich. This is a job for a detective inspector, not the local bobby. Telephone from your study so that you are not overheard.'

Markham shook his head in despair. His features clearly registering that he could not believe that all this mayhem and carnage was taking place beneath his roof.

'Go on, old chap. I'll stay here and have a sniff around, see if there are any clues to the demon who did this.'

Like an automaton, Algernon Markham made his way to the door and then turned. 'Send Doctor Locke up, you say,' he said faintly. To Wilde's surprise, he saw that he was crying.

Wilde nodded.

'Very well.' Markham heaved a heavy sigh and left.

Wilde wandered around the room but saw nothing of significance that would help in solving the crime. He observed a copy of Jonquil Callow's book of poems on the bedside table. Casually he picked it up and flicked through it. He observed the inscription Callow had written inside on the title page: 'To Cynara.' Now that is interesting, thought Wilde.

* * *

A few minutes later there was a gentle tap at the door and Doctor John Locke entered. 'Algernon said I should pop up and see the girl. Is she quite unwell?'

'Worse than that. I am afraid that she is dead.'

'What!'

'See for yourself.'

Locke crossed to the bed and Wilde pulled back the covers.

'My!' he said. 'This is all rather nasty.'

'I reckon these are similar to the wounds inflicted on Aubrey Sinclair. Same weapon, wouldn't you think, Doctor?'

'Mm, it is hard to say for certain but it looks…' Locke suddenly broke off. 'What is it?'

Locke had pulled the bedclothes further down revealing more of the body. 'There are three wounds to the chest area, and the killer has stabbed her twice in the stomach as well. Great heavens!'

Wilde rushed to Locke's side. 'Look,' the doctor hissed, 'two severe gashes here.'

Wilde gazed at the savage wounds. 'Whoever did this was determined that she wouldn't live.'

'I am afraid it was more than that, Mr Wilde. Feel her tummy.'

Wilde did as he was bidden, gently pressing his fingers down on the cold flesh. As he did so his eyes widened in shock. 'That is a definite bump. Great scot! Am I right in what I'm thinking?'

Locke nodded. 'Yes, it is clear to me that this girl was pregnant. The early stages, but this swelling clearly indicates that she was with child.'

Wilde felt a fierce chill run up his spine. 'If that is the case it can mean only one thing. This is a double murder: mother and child. Why else would the killer stab her so viciously in the stomach as well as the chest if not to destroy the growing baby as well as the mother?'

'I am afraid you are right. That is beyond horrible.'

Both men fell silent for some moments, gazing down at the poor mutilated creature that lay before them on the bed. Wilde found himself wondering what kind of foul beast could commit such a horrendous act. It was clear to him that the perpetrator of this atrocity must have known the girl well and that she was pregnant. The murder had been planned carefully and carried out in a cold-blooded fashion. This killer was a monster or mad – or both. But they did have a motive.

'This must remain our secret until the police arrive,' said Wilde at length. 'The awful truth is that someone in this house is the perpetrator of this terrible crime and that of the murder of Aubrey Sinclair. Someone we have socialised with; someone who wears a civilised, charming smile and hides a vicious heart of ice.'

Locke shook his head sadly. 'I believe you are right. I will be guided by you.'

'Cover the girl up and let's lock the door for the time being. We'll announce that she is just very poorly and you have given her some tablets…something like that, eh?'

Locke nodded. 'Yes. I think under the circumstances they will be less interested in an invalid than a murdered man.'

'Indeed, as old Thomas Gray had it: "ignorance is bliss."'

* * *

A solemn breakfast was taking place when the two men returned to the dining room. Markham had passed on the news of Aubrey Sinclair's murder, playing down the gory nature of the crime. The announcement and the fact that the police were to be contacted cast further gloom on the festivities and as a result conversation had been reduced to a minimum.

With unruffled efficiency Boldwood had rallied the staff, who had no knowledge of the dark tragedies that had occurred in the house, to serve the food that had been planned. Silverside had got his 'bangers and bacon' after all. He was tucking into his food with great relish apparently untouched by the news of Aubrey Sinclair's death.

Wilde and Locke joined the others at the table, each helping themselves to a small selection of food from the sideboard. Locke made his announcement concerning Stella Bond which was met with silence apart from a muted comment from Lady Julia: 'Poor girl.'

Wilde observed Sonia Lane toying with a small portion of scrambled eggs while staring blankly into space. No doubt the full extent of what had happened had gradually sunk in and instinctively her emotions were in turmoil. By contrast, Jonquil Callow seemed easy and relaxed. Having finished his food, he was sitting back in his chair puffing on a cigarette, watching the grey smoke curl upwards. He was no doubt, Wilde surmised, conjuring up one of his gloomy poems in which death and blood would feature.

The door opened and Algernon Markham entered. 'The police are on their way. They'll be here within the hour.'

Chapter Nine

The police did arrive an hour later in the form of Inspector Peter Craddock and Detective Sergeant Amos Brown. On making their way to Pelham House through the winding snowy lanes of Norfolk, they exchanged views on being called out to investigate a murder on Christmas Day.

Brown, a chubby, rosy-cheeked fellow with a neatly trimmed moustache, had been on duty that day and was moaning because he had been expecting a very easy shift. 'Christmas Day is usually as quiet as the grave, if you'll pardon the expression. Most folk, even the black-hearted felons, are at home stuffing their faces with turkey and pulling crackers,' he observed to his companion ruefully. 'I was looking forward to a few hours with my feet up at the station before I got home to the wife around eight to tuck into a late Christmas dinner. Now some devil goes and commits murder. Some people have no consideration.'

Inspector Craddock gave a tight grin. 'Well, to be honest, Sergeant, I'm relieved to be called out. It's bloody mayhem in my house. My brother-in-law and his wife are staying with us along with their two kids who don't get on with mine. Peace and goodwill are in short supply at Chez Craddock at the moment. A nice quiet murder seems all the more appealing.'

* * *

Meanwhile, Wilde had beckoned Kishen from the dining room into the hallway and brought him up-to-date concerning Stella Bond's murder.

'Gracious,' he said. 'What a tragedy. This place is turning into a charnel house. The poor lady, she was so young. She seemed such a nice person. When we talked, she told me she was keen to visit my country but that under her current circumstances that was unlikely...'

'Indeed. As an unmarried mother, she would have other concerns. That was why she was wearing those shapeless dresses to cover up the truth of her condition. And I believe there is more truth yet to be revealed.'

'I cannot help but feel so very sorry for the girl.'

'Indeed, so do I. No one deserves to die like that. It is important that you keep this piece of information under your hat for the moment, Kishen. I think we should let the police handle that.'

'Who do you think carried out these terrible crimes?'

'At this moment in time, with what slender evidence we have in our possession, it could be anyone. It's imperative that we establish a motive for each. It is clear to me that Stella's murder was deliberate. The killer intended that she and the baby she was carrying should die. Whereas Aubrey was out of his room in the corridor when he was attacked. It could be he was simply in the wrong place at the wrong time.'

'Explain please.'

'His room was next to Stella Bond's. He may well have heard noises from there and gone to investigate. He had his dressing gown on when he was found and I observed bloodstains between his room and the top of the stairs.'

Kishen's eyes widened. 'Ah, so you think he just wandered into the corridor and encountered the killer.'

Wilde nodded. 'Yes, that's how I read the matter. If he recognised the murderer...'

'Ah, I see.' Kishen's eyes glittered with excitement. 'So you believe that perhaps the poor fellow was stabbed simply to silence him—that was the motive.'

'Well, it's a theory. However, we need more data to confirm it, but it is useful to construct such ideas to see whether what we learn later strengthens them or blows them away.'

'I wonder who knew of Miss Bond's pregnancy.'

'Apart from the murderer, you mean? Good point. And who was the father of the child and did he know about the girl's pregnancy? She has been spending some time here at Pelham House, so maybe Aunt Julia suspected something. Women have an uncanny instinct about these kinds of things. Another aspect worth considering: if Stella intended to go it alone as a single mother she would soon have been in need of some cash. How was she going to manage?'

Kishen nodded. 'She certainly would have had to give up her job for a while.'

Wilde stroked his chin thoughtfully. 'I overheard her say to Markham that she would only give him until Boxing Day for something.'

'What?'

'Ah, well that is the question, as old Hamlet observed. It may be Algy has been a bit slow on passing over her dues. I know the old bird is a bit strapped for the readies. I've an inkling that's why Bertie the Brm Brm man is here.'

'Brm Brm man?'

'Motor cars. Brm Brm.'

'Oh, you mean Mr Silverside.'

'Eeh, by gum, I do.'

Both men laughed.

It wasn't long after this conversation took place between Wilde and Kishen that the police turned up on the doorstep of Pelham House. Kishen beat a hasty retreat back to his room, eager to escape into the fictional world of *David Copperfield* which appealed to him as being far more reassuring and less sensational than the real world of Pelham House with its bloody deeds and mysteries.

Boldwood took the two policemen into the library where they were joined by Algernon Markham, Doctor Locke, and Rupert Wilde, and introductions were made.

'Rupert Wilde, I know that name from somewhere,' said Craddock, peering closely at the young man. He'd met the type before; self-assured, elegantly dressed, monied, and no doubt as arrogant as a pig on holiday. Instinctively, he took an instant dislike to the fellow. 'Yes, yes, I remember now. You were in the papers. Something to do with a robbery or something. You were involved with the police... Scotland Yard.'

Wilde smiled indulgently. 'Yes. I assisted Detective Inspector Johnny Ferguson on ...'

'Of course,' interrupted Craddock excitedly, the pieces fitting into place. 'The Dobney tiara case. You were the amateur sleuth who managed to tie up the whole affair.'

'I just helped a little.'

'Oh, that's not what the police grapevine said. What about that, Brown? We have our own Sherlock Holmes on site. Perhaps, Mr Wilde, you'd like to tie up this case neatly, too, and then we can all go home.' There was a sharp edge of sarcasm to the Inspector's tone.

Wilde responded with a tolerant smile. 'I'm happy to lend a hand,' he said, lightly.

'Oh, I am sure you are,' observed the inspector tartly.

It was clear to Wilde that his offer to assist the inspector and his crony was taken begrudgingly. It was obvious that Craddock did not relish a pair of smart polished amateur shoes stomping down on his well-worn professional boots, but at the same time, he knew that if Craddock were astute enough he wouldn't reject any help that would help him reach a solution to this complicated case. Whatever, mused Wilde, I will have to tread carefully.

The body of Aubrey Sinclair was examined, Brown keeping his distance, his stomach not taking too kindly to the sight of blood.

'Well,' said Craddock, 'I am not a pathologist so I'm sure that I can deduce no more about this body than you gentlemen. It appears that several savage wounds were inflicted by some kind of blade, causing a loss of a great amount of blood and the victim's life. Is there anything else to learn at this stage, Doctor?'

Locke shook his head. 'I think your analysis sums it up.'

'Unfortunately, the pathologist is not going to be available until tomorrow when the body will be removed to HQ in Norwich, so we'll have to go with what we know so far. Now I think, Mr Markham, you'd better put us fully in the picture regarding the crime, the victim, and the other parties present in this house at the moment.

'Indeed, Inspector. Perhaps it would be best if we move to my study away from any unpleasant distractions.' He cast a wary eye over the bloody corpse. 'And I am sure I can get Boldwood to provide us with coffee.'

'That would be grand,' said Brown.

Once they were settled in the study, Algernon recounted in a somewhat hesitant fashion the events of the last twenty-four hours. Brown scribbled down all the details, including what he considered was a cast list of suspects. After reaching the point where Boldwood discovered the body, Markham paused and slumped back in his chair as though recounting the events thus far had sapped all his strength.

'So,' said the inspector, 'it would seem that Sinclair's wife...Sonia...' He glanced over at Brown.

'Lane,' came the reply after the sergeant had checked his notebook.

'Yes, this Sonia Lane is the key suspect in this matter.'

'That maybe so, but I'm afraid the story does not end there,' said Wilde.

'Oh?'

'There has been another murder.'

Craddock said nothing but his mouth gaped a little.

'Another murder,' repeated Brown, checking that he had heard correctly.

Wilde nodded in confirmation.

'Two bodies overnight. That is going a bit far, isn't it?' observed Craddock wryly. 'In fact, I'm beginning to feel a little unsafe myself. Well, you'd better fill me in on the second murder.'

Wilde took up the thread this time and recounted the discovery of Stella Bond's corpse and the fact that she was in the early stages of pregnancy.

'Goodness,' said Craddock rubbing his chin, 'you don't do things by halves at Pelham House, do you. So, we have Aubrey Sinclair and Stella Bond both stabbed last night. Apart from the fact they were guests at your house party, Mr Markham, do you know of any connection between these two people?'

Markham shook his head. 'No, as far I know they had not met before arriving here yesterday afternoon.

'And how do you know them?'

'Stella has been working at the house, cataloguing and valuing my art collection.'

'You have a lot of pictures then?' asked Brown.

'I have a gallery of paintings, yes.'

'And why are you having them catalogued and valued?' Craddock enquired.

Markham frowned. 'This is going a little off the mark, isn't it?'

'It would help if you would just answer the question, sir,' came the stern rebuff.

'I'm planning to sell a few of the less significant paintings to help with the maintenance of my home. I hope that satisfies you.'

Craddock gave him the cool eye. 'For the moment. Am I right in thinking that you have kept the news of this second death from the rest of the guests?'

'Indeed, Inspector,' said Doctor Locke. 'We thought it best...'

Craddock pursed his lips. 'You were probably right. And what about Sinclair? How do you come to know him? I gather he's a playwright.'

'Yes, had a lot of stuff in the West End,' said Markham. 'It is my wife who knows him, knew him better than I. She moves in arty circles, you understand.'

Craddock nodded, but his expression clearly indicated that he did not really understand such a concept. It was referring to a world far removed from his own.

'We've been in their company—Sonia and Aubrey—at various parties and dined with them a few times, but I cannot say they were firm friends of ours—just pleasant acquaintances, if you like.'

Craddock glanced over at Brown to check that he had noted the main points of Markham's statement and then rose quickly from his chair. 'Well, gentlemen, I think we should have a look at the second victim.'

The men trooped in silent procession up to Stella Bond's bedroom. Again it was Craddock who took a close look at the body and the wounds while Brown stayed well back from the blood-soaked bed.

'This attack seems far more savage,' Craddock said. 'Would you agree, Doctor?'

'I am afraid so.'

'And you are convinced that the girl was pregnant. This swelling…it's not just fat?'

'The bump is too firm and too high to just be belly fat. Of course, you'll need a post-mortem to be absolutely sure, but I am convinced in my own mind.'

'That fact could easily affect the complexion of this murder. Was the girl killed because she was with child?'

'It may well have been someone who didn't want the world to know this unmarried girl was pregnant,' said Wilde.

'Like the father you mean?'

'That would be the obvious thought,' agreed Wilde.

'So could one of your guests be the daddy, Mr Markham?' asked Craddock.

Markham's face turned white at this suggestion. 'Of course not. They are all respectable individuals.'

'Not all that respectable, sir. At least one of them is a murderer.'

Chapter Ten

In the kitchen, Lady Julia was in conference with Boldwood and Florence Daley, the cook. Julia sat opposite Mrs Daley by the large kitchen table, while Boldwood stood some distance away, like a dark, erect sentinel.

'Despite the terrible upheaval and great tragedy that has occurred, we still have a duty to feed our guests,' Lady Julia said gravely. 'So we must go ahead with our Christmas lunch more or less as planned. We will serve it a little later than scheduled, sometime around mid-afternoon, and try to make it as pleasant as possible. Are there any problems with that arrangement, Mrs Daley?'

The cook shook her head. 'No, madam. The food is all prepared and ready for the oven. I'll just go ahead as normal.'

'There you are, my lady, it was as I intimated. All is under control regarding the festive luncheon,' observed Boldwood.

Lady Julia sighed. 'Thank heaven. It is a small blessing, but a blessing nonetheless.'

'Should I set places for the two gentlemen from the police?' asked the butler.

Lady Julia frowned. 'Well, I suppose you'd better. It's not the ideal situation to have two detectives eyeing us all up as we pass the cranberry jelly and eat our turkey.'

Before Boldwood could respond, the door of the kitchen burst open and one of the maids entered. Her face was flushed and her eyes wild with excitement.

'Gracious, girl,' said Boldwood, 'what on earth's the matter?'

'It's in the conservatory…'

'What is?'

'The door…' She hesitated, seeming to lose track of what she was saying.

Lady Julia stepped forward and placed her hand on the girl's shoulder. 'Take a deep breath, Nancy, and then try to explain yourself sensibly.'

The girl did as she was told, inhaling wheezily, before continuing. 'I went into the conservatory just now to tidy up and dust as is my usual practice and I found …' Here she paused again as though she had lost the power to describe what she had found.

'Come on, girl,' said Boldwood, not unkindly. 'Speak up.'

'The French windows have been opened and…one of the panes has been smashed. It looks like we've had burglars.'

Lady Julia shot a concerned glance at Boldwood. 'What now!' she sighed. 'The policemen need to be informed of this development. Would you do that, Boldwood?'

'Of course, madam.'

* * *

Ten minutes later, Inspector Craddock and Detective Sergeant Brown, accompanied by Algernon Markham and Rupert Wilde, were shown into the conservatory situated at the rear of the house. Dr Locke had absented himself from this excursion in favour of a 'lunchtime pick me up.' 'It's been a hell of a morning. I need some stimulation,' he explained.

The conservatory was awash with ferns and cane furniture. The windows looked out on a stretch of snow-bedecked lawn and the flat rolling country-side beyond. One of the French windows was ajar and flapping in an errant fashion in the stiff breeze that filled the room with an Arctic chill. One of the panes was missing with fragments of glass scattered on the carpet nearby.

'So there has been an intruder in the house,' announced Markham, with a note of relief in his voice.

'It certainly looks like it,' said Brown. 'This changes the complexion of the case, doesn't it?'

'It appears so,' muttered Craddock absentmindedly as he examined the door along with Wilde.

'Is it all right if I arrange for the mess to be cleared up, Inspector?' asked Markham.

''Fraid not, sir. I'll need to get the fingerprints boys onto this first. Don't want things contaminated by other prints. Could cause a lot of confusion.' The inspector took a handkerchief from his pocket, wound it around his hand, and gently pushed the door closed. 'That will have to do for the time being. This room is now off-limits.'

'Very well.'

'Now, Mr Markham, I would like to commandeer your study as the interview room.'

'Anything you say, Inspector.'

'Good. Give me fifteen minutes or so and then I'll start having a chat with your guests. See if we can't throw some light into the darkness.'

'Very well, but in the meantime, if you'll excuse me, I have some domestic arrangements to attend to. Lunch and things. Certain aspects still have to proceed you know, despite ... what has happened. It is Christmas Day after all and I have guests to consider. You will be most welcome to dine with us.'

Before Craddock could respond, Brown chipped in with a cheery, 'That is most kind, sir.'

'Our pleasure. The luncheon gong will sound at three pm.' Markham gave a tight smile and left the room. Wilde was about to follow him when Craddock touched his arm.

'Just a moment, Mr Wilde. I wonder if you'd mind sitting in on the interviews. I think it could be very useful to us. Because of your police experience and more particularly the fact that you've been in the house during the time the crimes were committed and observed the guests. Your take on their responses and versions of events could help give us a clearer picture. You may be able to provide a different perspective on things and spot any anomalies that guests make in their statements.'

'Of course. As I mentioned earlier, I'm happy to help if I can, Inspector, but...'

'But?'

'Well, there's just one thing: are you so sure that I'm not the killer?'

* * *

Kishen lay on his bed with his copy of *David Copperfield* but found that the words on the page blurred before his eyes. He could not concentrate on the text. His mind was awhirl with thoughts regarding the dark events that had taken place in the last twenty-four hours. In the end, he admitted defeat, placed the novel down on the bedside cabinet, and extracted a note pad from his valise. He wrote down a list of all the guests in the house and began to consider their eligibility as a murder suspect. He cudgelled his brain but found he was making no progress. The real problem was the motive. Who would want to kill Aubrey Sinclair and Stella Bond? What was the connection between them? He tried desperately to conjure up a motive that would link the two victims, but he failed. And where did Jonquil Callow fit into the scheme of things? How did Stella know that blue cufflink belonged to him... unless she had seen it before? She was an observant lady—that was part of her job. However, Kishen could not imagine the effete poet wielding a knife, or was he just being naïve? And then there was that bluff businessman, Silverside. Kishen instinctively felt wary of him. He wondered if this fellow, who insisted on being called Bertie, was all that he seemed to be or what he wanted you to think he was. Of course, he could be merely like himself: just an innocent bystander.

All these thoughts fluttered around Kishen's brain to no effect. It was all incoherent guesswork at best. With a frustrated groan, he tore the page from his notepad and screwed it up, depositing it in the wastepaper basket. He admitted defeat. He had no idea who committed the murders or why. He had to admit that he was no detective. He would have to leave all that to Rupert Wilde.

Chapter Eleven

In the study, Craddock and Brown sat behind the desk, a chair placed before them for the interviewee, while Wilde was sitting in the shadowed corner of the room in a comfortable wing chair.

'There is one thing that I think you ought to know,' said Wilde casually as he lit up a cigarette. 'There has been no intruder in the house. That broken French window was a setup, created to mislead.'

Craddock raised an eyebrow. 'What makes you say that?'

'Didn't you notice the snow outside in close proximity to the window?'

Craddock paused and then shook his head.

'Anyone standing outside the window to break in would have left marks in the snow. There were none. It was pristine. Someone has tried to create the impression of an intruder breaking into the conservatory to focus attention away from the guests. It is clear to me that the glass was broken by someone inside the house. Notice how you managed to close the window. It had not been locked.'

Craddock and Brown exchanged glances and then the inspector sported a reluctant grin. 'Quite the Sherlock Holmes, aren't we, Mr Wilde?'

'Good bit of detective work,' enthused Brown.

Craddock threw the sergeant a dark glance. 'So', said the inspector, 'we are left with the situation as before. The killer is one of the inmates.'

'That is how I read the riddle,' observed Wilde, puffing gently on his cigarette. 'So it's our job to softly, softly, catchee monkey.'

'Quite,' said Craddock, not too happy with the phrase 'our job, but he let it pass. 'Well, let's have a chat with all of them. With a bit of luck, the guilty party will make some kind of fatal slip. Pick a name off the list, Brown, and we'll make a start.'

'How about Bertram Silverside,' said Brown.

'Fine. Please go and rouse him. In the meantime, perhaps you can give us the low down on this feller, Mr Wilde.'

* * *

Bertram 'Bertie' Silverside beamed with amusement at the inspector as he took the seat opposite him. 'Crikey,' he said, 'it's like being back at school is this. Hauled up before the headmaster for being a naughty boy. Are you going to confiscate my catapult and give me six of the best?'

'Were you a naughty boy?' asked Craddock without humour.

'I was a healthy, normal lad—and I continue to be so. Now then what d'you need to know?'

'Well, let's start with how you came to be here, to be spending Christmas at Pelham House.'

'Because I was invited. Algernon Markham asked me.'

'How do you know him?'

'Well, if the truth be known, I don't actually 'know him' as such. He's really only an acquaintance. We met at a picture sale some months ago. I bought one of his landscapes. A small study of Ullswater by Arnold Mellor. Not a masterpiece, you understand, but it took my fancy. Markham and I fell into conversation after the sale and we had drinks together. We seemed to rub along nicely. He's a decent enough bloke. I invited him to visit me at my factory and I gave him the royal tour. It was after this that he asked me to his Christmas house party so's I could take a look at his painting collection. He's trying to get me to buy a few more.'

'And are you going to?' asked Wilde from the shadows.

Silverside turned abruptly. He hadn't noticed him in the corner.

'Oh, it's you. You're the spectre at the feast, are you? Special constable are we now?'

'More a fly on the wall,' remarked Wilde casually.

'Well, in answer to your question I'm not sure, but if I'm honest with you…'

'It would be best,' observed Craddock.

'Well, on the QT, old Algernon has got me down here to tap me for a loan. A considerable loan. I'm afraid he seems to be in the mire financially and he sees me as a bit of a cash cow.'

'Has he asked you outright for some cash?'

Silverside nodded in the affirmative. 'Aye, he has.'

'How much?'

'If you must know…it was five thousand pounds.'

Brown gave a low whistle.

'Have you agreed to the loan?' Wilde enquired.

'I am quite aware that I have a rough and ready exterior, but I assure you I have a sharp brain and a keen eye. I didn't achieve the success I've had by being a fool with my money or a soft touch. I like Algernon, he's a decent chap as far as I can tell, and I feel sorry for him but I'm not about to chuck him five grand. I know he's offered some of the paintings as collateral but I don't want to be bothered with all that malarkey. It's cash for cash with me. I've told him so.'

'How did he take it?'

Silverside gave a dark chuckle. 'Not well I'm afraid. He wasn't expecting a rejection and he's still persevering, but when Bertie Silverside says no, he means no. But all this has got nothing to do with the murder has it?'

'All information helps us to build up a picture of what went on here in the last twenty-four hours, Mr Silverside. Sometimes information that appears trivial and incidental can, in the end, have a great bearing on events,' observed Craddock.

Silverside shook his head. 'I can't see how my dealings with Markham can have any connection with the death of that Sinclair chap.'

'Have you any thoughts or theories about the murder?'

'Not really. It seems to me after that bit of nonsense last evening with his wife accusing him of trying to poison her, she would be the most likely culprit to do him in. She's obviously a neurotic piece. Theatrical as well. That farrago at the dinner table could have easily tipped her over the edge.'

'Did you hear anything during the night? Noises, voices?'

'I slept like a top. We folk with clear consciences do, you know. Head on pillow—out like a light.'

'What do you make of the other guests: Doctor Locke, Jonquil Callow, and Stella Bond?'

'Don't make much of them, if the truth be told. I mean I only met them yesterday and have barely exchanged more than a few sentences with any of them. Locke seems a decent enough fellow. But Callow…well I can't be doing with airy fairy folk. He tried to sell me one of his poetry books. I told him the only reading I do is the *Financial Times* and the odd western novel. Can't be doing with sentimental rhyming stuff. That's for ladies with an over-sensitive imagination.'

'How did he react when you refused to buy his book?'

Silverside grinned. 'At first, he looked shocked and then indignant. He just said "Well!" and flounced off. He's a bit of a pansy if you ask me.'

'I saw you in conversation with Miss Bond,' said Wilde. 'What did you think about her?'

'She seems a nice lass. Rather pretty behind those big glasses. Bit on the serious side though. A smile would help her a lot.'

'What did you talk about?' asked Wilde.

'She was interested in whether I was going to buy any of Markham's paintings. She seemed very disappointed, angry even, when I told her I wasn't.'

'You seem to be making a habit of disappointing people, sir,' observed Brown, looking up from his notebook.

'I speak my mind, if that's what you mean. There's no point in being any other way.'

Wilde acknowledged this bluff statement with a brief nod and returned to the subject of Stella Bond. 'What did you make of her desire for you to purchase one of Markham's pictures?'

'I don't know that I made anything of it. I reckon she was trying to add a bit of persuasive pressure on his behalf. I got the impression that she's fond of the fellow and no doubt is aware of his financial position. Well, she has been working here on and off for some time so she was probably hoping I'd help him out, which I suppose in turn would help her out and justify her efforts. But as I intimated earlier: I'm not a charity case.'

'You say you thought she was 'fond of the fellow? How did you make that out?' asked Craddock.

'Just an impression. She looked a bit doe-eyed when she mentioned his name. Perhaps she was hoping he'd turn out to be her sugar daddy.'

'That's quite a serious accusation.'

'Oh, I'm not serious. It was just a thought. I've no reason…' Silverside broke off and gave a big sigh. 'The truth is I've no facts to offer you that will help in your investigations, so, gentlemen, are we done? There's a glass of whisky and soda in the drawing room with my name on it.'

* * *

'Well,' said Detective Sergeant Brown expansively after Silverside had left the room, 'Mr Silverside didn't exhibit any signs that he knew Stella Bond is dead.'

'Or it was a performance,' remarked Craddock.

'Indeed,' agreed Wilde. 'Old Bertie enjoys playing the bluff northerner who has so much money he feels he can say or do what he likes and get away with it.'

'Like murder?' said Brown.

Chapter Twelve

Jonquil Callow was the next guest in the study. He sat on the same seat that had just been vacated by Bertram Silverside. Callow seemed nervous and adopted a rather hunched posture with his knees close together, his head craning forward, the floppy hair dangling just above his eyebrows.

'I can tell you from the start,' he said, his wavering voice moving into a higher register than normal, 'I know nothing. I have no idea who is responsible for the murders...'

'Murders?' challenged Craddock.

'Sorry, did I say murders, I meant murder. I suppose I was thinking about last night's dinner when Sonia collapsed after accusing her husband of trying to kill her.'

'What do you make of it all?'

Jonquil looked blankly at the Inspector. 'Nothing, really. Do *you* believe that someone in this house killed that nasty little playwright?'

'We're only at the start of our investigation, Mr Callow. It is too soon to reach such a conclusion, but I suppose it is most likely.'

Callow shuddered. 'Horrible thought. Of course, it could have been one of the servants.'

'What would be their motive?'

'Search me. What motive can any of us have—except of course his wife. She might well have wanted to get her own back.'

'Is that how you see it?'

'Now you're trying to put words in my mouth. I told you already I've no idea.'

'You referred to Aubrey Sinclair just now as "that nasty little playwright". That's quite a harsh description. How did you reach this view of him?' Craddock asked.

'Because he was very rude to me. I tried to sell him one of my poetry books and he said something quite upsetting to me.'

'What was that?'

Callow looked over at Brown. 'I trust you're not going to put this in your little notebook.'

'It's my duty, sir,' replied Brown. 'It could be used in evidence later.'

Callow's eyes widened. 'Oh, I sincerely hope not.'

'Come now, Mr Callow, what did Sinclair say to you?' prompted Craddock.

'I offered him one of my poetry books. He just looked at it with disdain and said, 'Get lost, you damned fairy.''

'What did you say to that?'

'What could one say? I just turned around and walked away.'

'Did it anger you?'

'Of course, it did. It was not only an insult to my talent...but cast aspersions on my sexuality. I'd have liked to ram my book down his uncouth throat.' Callow's cheeks coloured now with emotion and he wriggled uncomfortably on his chair.

'I expect at that particular moment you really hated "that nasty little playwright,"' suggested Brown.

'You bet I did. I could...' Callow paused. 'Oh, no you don't, putting words into my mouth again. You wanted me to say that I could have killed him or something to that effect. Well, maybe I was full of animosity for a few seconds, but I didn't murder the creep. He wasn't worth the effort.'

'I don't think the sergeant was suggesting such a thing or trying to elicit a confession out you.'

'Well, he'd be very disappointed if he was.'

'Let's move on. What do you make of Stella Bond?'

This question seemed to disturb the poet and he hesitated before replying. 'She seems a very pleasant girl, I suppose.'

'You mean she bought one of your books,' observed Wilde with a hint of mischief in his voice.

Callow pursed his lips. 'As a matter of fact, I gave her a copy. "I always support the arts," she had told me and offered to buy one but I let her have one for free as I did with you, Mr Wilde.'

'Did you discuss the arts with her? Markham's paintings for example.'

'Not in any detail. I asked her when she was going to have done working at the house and she said a strange thing: "By Boxing Day if he's not bloody careful". It was an off-hand remark. She said it as though she was talking to herself.'

'What do you think she meant by that?'

'Your guess is as good as mine.'

'You didn't ask her?'

'I didn't think it was my place. It's something you can raise with her yourself.'

At this moment there was a gentle knock at the door.

'Come in,' Craddock called out and Boldwood entered, carrying a tray containing a large coffee pot, cream jug, and crockery. 'Lady Julia thought you might appreciate a cup of coffee, gentlemen,' he said in his usual sepulchral tones.

'That's very decent of her,' said Craddock, rising from his chair. 'Put the tray on the desk. We can serve ourselves.'

'If you are sure, sir?'

'Yes, yes.' And then turning to Jonquil Callow. 'I think that will be all for now, Mr Callow, unless you can think of anything that would throw more light on the case.'

'No. Nothing at all. I find the whole thing horrible and baffling. Quite honestly, I just want to leave this dreadful house and return home.'

'That will not be possible for the moment, I'm afraid. Thank you for your cooperation.'

The poet gave a heavy sigh, rose quickly, and fled the room as though he was being chased by a pack of savage hounds. The two policemen exchanged amused glances.

'Will there be anything else?' enquired Boldwood, moving slowly backwards towards the door.

'Yes. Could you inform Miss Sonia Lane we'd like to have a word with her in here.'

'Of course, sir.'

'Brown, will you be mother?' said Craddock after the butler had gone sliding out of the room like a ghost. 'I'll take my coffee with three sugars and cream. What about you, Mr Wilde?'

'Just black, please,' came the reply.

'Well, Mr Wilde, what d'you make of it so far?' said Craddock some moments later as he sat back in his chair sipping his sweet cup of coffee.

Wilde grinned. 'Well, I'm fairly certain it's not the butler.'

Brown guffawed.

Craddock, not amused, persevered. 'The key question is who do you suspect?'

'All we have at present are jigsaw pieces, not enough to slot together to create any part of the picture. Unless, of course, you've got a culprit in mind.'

'If I have, that's where they are staying for the moment,' observed Craddock pointedly.

'Very wise, if I may say so. Let's carry on for the moment and see what other nuggets we dig up.'

Sonia Lane arrived moments later in a very dramatic fashion. The door swung open but there was no one in the aperture at first and then suddenly she appeared. Her arms flung wide as though she were releasing a pair of doves into the room.

She stepped forward, her eyes ablaze, her red lips trembling. 'I gather you wish to see me,' she announced in husky tones.

'Indeed we do,' said Craddock, somewhat taken aback by this theatrical entrance. Here before him was a mixture of Lady Macbeth and Cleopatra and he was intimidated by her presence.

He jumped up, rushed round the desk, and guided her to the seat before it.

She gave him a brief nod of gratitude. 'Before you start bombarding me with questions, I wish to make a statement,' she announced imperiously, smoothing down her dress. 'My marriage to Aubrey has been in difficulties for some time. I saw over the years the warm, kind man I married turn into a cold-hearted, cruel individual. To say that we had drifted apart would be an understatement. It was as though we were on different oceans. It is true that on occasion I sought comfort and affection elsewhere. Who wouldn't under the circumstances? I am only human after all. I am sure no right-minded person could criticise me for my actions. And, believe me, Aubrey made me pay for my "dalliances," as he called them. He ill-used me at times, both mentally and physically. In recent months I became convinced that he wanted rid of me. On more than one occasion he actually threatened to kill me...'

At this point, Craddock leaned forward and was about to ask a question regarding this statement, but Sonia raised her hand to silence him.

'I am in no way going to go into details about this. You will have to take my word for it for the moment until I have consulted my solicitor. But I believe there was a serious threat to my life hanging over me and so last night when I tasted my wine, I was convinced that the devil was trying to poison me.'

'There I must stop you, Miss Lane,' said Wilde from the shadows.

She turned suddenly in his direction as though she had not noticed him before.

'I beg your pardon,' she said.

'Here we are veering from the truth, I'm afraid. You see I know that you planted the poison in the drink yourself—although, of course, it wasn't poison—just a harmless mixture of bitter almonds meant to create the impression that it was cyanide. It was a ploy of yours to implicate your husband for attempted murder. No doubt you wished to prompt a scandal that would help to make a divorce so much easier to obtain, while, at the same time, creating unpleasant repercussions for Aubrey as a form of revenge for his cruelty towards you.'

At first, Sonia Lane seemed shocked by Wilde's accusation, but she managed to contain her unease, stating, 'I don't know what on earth you are talking about.'

'I found the phial of the concoction you added to your drink in your handbag.'

'Great heavens, is this true?' asked Craddock.

Sonia Lane sat back in the chair and gave a wry smile. 'Well, it seems futile to deny it. I just meant the old buzzard to get into trouble for a while. To put the wind up him, if you like. Of course, I knew the case wouldn't hold water. The wine would be tested and found to be harmless. It was just a shot across his bows.'

Craddock rolled his eyes.

'And now if I may continue my statement…I am well aware that because of the animosity between me and my husband I would appear to be the obvious suspect for his murder, but I can assure you that I did not kill him. Why should I? I have enough sense to realise that I would become the obvious culprit. Only a fool would do that. And, I can assure you, I am no fool. If I wanted him dead, and I didn't really, I just wanted rid of him, surely I would arrange for his demise to take place when I wasn't in the vicinity and in a less dramatic manner. Certainly not during a house party at Christmas.' She paused to draw breath and then began again. 'Also, I had been given a strong sleeping draught by Doctor Locke and I was out like a light. I couldn't have dragged myself up in the middle of the night, found a knife, and then somehow lured Aubrey onto the landing to stab him. I didn't even know which room he was in.'

'That's all very convincing,' observed Craddock, but got no further.

'Of course, it is convincing because it's the truth,' she exclaimed with an indignant roar.

'Then who do you suspect of murdering your husband?'

Sonia Lane gave a dramatic shrug of the shoulders. 'How the hell do I know? That's your job, isn't it?'

'How many people amongst the guests had your husband met before yesterday?' asked Wilde, lighting another cigarette.

Sonia thought for a moment. 'Well, as far as I know, it was just Julia and Algy. The rest were strangers. At least they were to me and Aubrey didn't mention that he'd encountered any of the others before.'

'You've admitted that during your marriage you had liaisons. Did your husband also?'

'I don't really know. It's possible but I had no evidence of it. Mind you, I didn't go looking for it. He could have been having an affair with a whole line of chorus boys from the Palladium for all I knew, I really wouldn't have cared.'

There followed an awkward silence. Craddock sat back in his chair and stroked his chin. 'Chorus boys, you say.'

'Yes, you heard me. Aubrey had a leaning in that direction. I didn't find out until after we were married.'

'So,' said Wilde, 'was that the reason there was animosity between you?'

'One of the reasons. He could be violent, too, especially when in drink. We put up a bloody good front in public, famous actress and successful playwright, but behind the scenes it was rough.' She gave a sour smile, adding, 'To be honest I think I gave a better performance as a dutiful wife than I ever did on the West End stage.'

'Do you know of any of his men friends who may have had a grudge against him?' asked Craddock.

Sonia gave a dry, mirthless chuckle. 'You mean a spurned lover.'

Craddock coloured a little. 'Something like that.'

'Are you suggesting someone travelled down to Norfolk, struggled through the snow, and hid in the house until he got the opportunity to stab my husband and then disappeared into the night? Don't be ridiculous, Inspector.'

Craddock looked suitably miffed.

'Is there anything you can tell us that you consider may have some bearing on this case?'

'Not that I can think of. I know that I have given you the impression that I am something of a hard-bitten, vindictive woman. Struggling in an unpleasant marriage can do that to a person. However, I will say that however much I grew to dislike my husband, hate him even, I would not go to the lengths of murdering him. And I am sad at his departing. We were happy once and no one deserves to die like he did.' Her eyes moistened now.

Wilde couldn't make up his mind whether this was genuine emotion or just part of her performance. Well, he mused, she is a bloody good actress and it seemed now she was getting ready for her curtain call.

'May I go now? I am in desperate need of fortifying with a large gin and tonic.'

'Certainly, madam,' said Craddock deferentially. 'Thank you for your time.'

After she had left, Craddock heaved a large sigh. 'Phew, that is some strong lady. I certainly wouldn't like to get on the wrong side of her.'

'But is she murderer material?' asked Brown.

'My instinct says not in this case. She spoke a lot of sense in defence of herself. However, in truth, the jury is still out. At present, she is the one with the strongest motive – or the strongest motive that we are aware of. What do you think Mr Wilde?'

'My thoughts are the same as yours, Inspector. She did make a very pertinent point when she said that if she'd wanted to bump the old boy off, she certainly wouldn't have chosen to do it at a fairly intimate house party. Now if Aubrey had really tried to poison her last night, it could be argued that such an event may well have affected her emotionally and thus driven her to seek revenge; but as the poisoning farrago was of her own design that is unlikely to be the case. In fact, it shows she had cold nerve and was in full control of her emotions.'

'Right you are, Mr Wilde.' Craddock glanced at his watch. 'Apparently, lunch is in half an hour, I think we've just got time to interview Doctor Locke before grub is up. Then we'll have covered all the inmates.'

'Not quite. There are our hosts and my assistant Kishen.'

'Well, I am sure you can vouch for him.'

'Maybe, but I think he should be allowed to give his view of events.'

'Very well, if you think that would be useful. After lunch, maybe. Now, Brown, will you see if you can round up Doctor Locke.'

* * *

'You're fairly new to the neighbourhood I gather, Doctor Locke?' began Craddock after the doctor had settled himself down casually on the chair opposite the desk.

'That's right. I've been in the village just a little over six months.'

'You seemed to have settled in quite nicely—being invited up to the big house for the Christmas celebrations.'

'I suppose so. Both Lady Julia and Algernon are my patients. So I have been visiting them here on a regular basis for consultations.'

'I see. What have you been treating them for?'

Locke gave a gentle frown. 'I can't break the patients' confidentiality, Inspector. You must be aware of that.'

'This is a murder enquiry. I need to know all the facts.'

'Facts that are relevant to the crime, yes, but I'm sure the information you have just requested has no bearing on the murders that have taken place here.'

'That is my place to judge, not yours.'

'Surely you can't be suggesting that either Julia or Algernon are involved, implicated in the deaths of Aubrey Sinclair and Stella Bond?'

'I am neither suggesting nor denying such a thing. I am merely trying to establish the facts and it is your duty as a responsible citizen to help the police with their enquiries. So I repeat again, what have you been treating your hosts for?'

Locke pursed his lips with annoyance. 'Very well,' he said at length. 'Lady Julia suffers from insomnia and high blood pressure, which needs to be monitored regularly and Algernon has occasional attacks of gout. Satisfied with that?'

Craddock glanced over at Brown to check that he had recorded those details.

'Satisfied. For the moment, at least. Now, Doctor, have you seen or heard anything since you arrived at the house which might make you suspect any of the guests…?'

'Well, if I'd known what was going to happen, I'd have kept my eyes peeled and my ears open, but I was here for what I hoped would be a jolly relaxing festive occasion. All the guests are strangers to me and, while I have formed simple opinions about them, I have no knowledge of their connections and hold no deep insight into their characters or motives. I'm just a plain GP, not a psychiatrist. I'm afraid I don't see anyone as being a murderer.'

'Please share these "simple opinions."'

'You're intent on squeezing this lemon dry, aren't you? Very well, regarding the surviving guests, I would say that they are all pleasant enough in their own way but if pressed I would suggest: Silverside, self-satisfied; Callow, somewhat pompous and self-centred; Mr Wilde here—rather enigmatic. I have no thoughts on the Indian chappie, Mr Wilde's secretary. Not having been in conversation with him. Seems a shy young man.'

'And Sonia Lane?' added Craddock.

'Ah, well she is an interesting case. On the surface, she appears a strong and determined woman, but I think that indomitable suit of armour she wears is very fragile. Underneath, I believe she is a sensitive and very vulnerable lady. But, as I say, I'm no shrink. It's just my opinion. Will that do?'

Before Craddock could reply, Wilde leaned forward with a question. 'On your visits to the house to attend on Julia and Algernon, did you ever encounter Stella Bond.'

Locke seemed surprised at this query. 'Er no, not that I can recall. If she was around she'd be in another part of the house, the picture gallery probably.' He shook his head gently. 'I have no memory of seeing her before yesterday.'

Suddenly there came the sound of a booming gong.

'Ah, lunch,' exclaimed Locke with enthusiasm. 'I am starving. Well, not really, it is a commonly used phrase but inaccurate. What I mean to say is that I am somewhat hungry and I would like to eat. Have we finished?'

'For the moment. Thank you, Doctor.'

Without another word, he left the room.

'Any thoughts?' asked Craddock.

Wilde gave a light laugh. 'Well, as the enigmatic one here, I would enroll Doctor Locke as a member of my club. He's a difficult fellow to fathom.'

The gong reverberated once more.

'I think we'd better go and tackle a morsel of turkey,' observed Wilde. 'Let's just allow a little Christmas to intrude; a pleasant interval before investigations are resumed.'

Craddock sighed. 'I suppose so.'

Chapter Thirteen

To Wilde's mind, the Christmas lunch was certainly no 'pleasant interval.' Indeed it was like a dreary wake. The gaily coloured crackers that lay by each place were left untouched. No one thought it appropriate to pull them, creating a feeble bang and donning a silly paper hat. The festive table decorations seemed to mock the occasion. Jollity was banished. No one wished another a 'Merry Christmas.' Death had spread its gloomy pall over the household.

Bertie Silverside seemed the only relaxed diner at the table, apparently unaffected by what had occurred in the environs of Pelham House. There he was stuffing his face with glazed ham, beef, turkey, and all the trimmings, dabbing his greasy chin at regular intervals with his napkin to mop up the excess juices.

Jonquil Callow, loured over his plate, nibbling his food like an effete rabbit. He was careful not to look about him in an effort to avoid catching anyone's eye. It was as though he wished to create his own bubble that isolated himself from all the other diners. To Wilde, he gave the impression of wishing to remove himself from the horrid reality of dining in a house where murders have been committed. Maybe it was just an impression.

Lady Julia kept glancing around the room nervously, examining the faces of her guests. Wilde wondered whether she was pondering which one of them might be a murderer or just hoping the lunch was providing some kind of divertissement from thoughts of the grim occurrences during the night. For the most part, Algernon was staring into space, taking only the occasional mouthful. Despite his claims to be hungry, Doctor Locke also ate sparingly while attempting to engage Sonia Lane in conversation. As far as Wilde could make out his attempts were far from successful as she appeared to respond in muttered monosyllables, while she played with her food. The theatrical bravado she had demonstrated earlier seemed to have dissipated. Wilde wondered what on earth was on her mind. It was ironic that as an actress she had experienced the most dramatic of times in the last twenty-four hours from her own improvised performance as a poison victim to the brutal murder of her husband. Had she brought about his demise and actually stabbed him to death? For a split second, he conjured up an image in his mind of a shadowy figure wielding the weapon—the bloody knife. The knife! Ah, yes. Suddenly a thought struck him. He made a mental note: that was something he must check later.

Wilde's gaze drifted to the two policemen, hunkered up together at the far corner of the table. They ate heartily enough, but he could see from their uneasy expressions that they were far from relaxed. Apart from any feelings of discomfort at having to take Christmas lunch with a group of strangers, they were also aware that one of these diners sitting at the same table devouring the flesh of dead creatures was likely to have committed two murders. Wilde did not envy their situation.

'How is the investigation going?' came a muted voice at his side. Wilde gave Kishen a gentle raise of the eyebrow. 'All the balls are in the air at the moment,' he said *sotto voce*. 'Who have you placed your money on?'

'Me? Gracious, I have no idea. I have tried to work it all out but to no avail. Murder is a terrible act. I believe in order to commit it one must possess an element of madness. One must lose one's natural senses and slip into a very dark place. Looking around the table, I can see no glimpses of cruel madness in the eyes of anyone.'

'Ah, but the cunning killer can conceal the madness. The trick is to uncover it.'

'And so you are going to assume the role of the master conjuror and with a wave of your magic wand expose the madness.'

'Well, I'm going to try.'

There was a sudden clatter of cutlery at the opposite side of the table. Bernie

Silverside had dropped his knife and fork onto his plate with a flourish. 'Well, Lady Julia, that was a grand meal. There's nothing like a Norfolk turkey; succulent and rich. I presume it was a Norfolk turkey?'

Julia nodded. 'Yes, yes, from a local farm.' She attempted a smile, but the lips didn't quite make it.

Now Silverside turned his attention to the policemen. 'Tell me, Inspector, how long are you going to be here and how long do we have to stay in Pelham House? I have important meetings in London on the 27th.'

Craddock looked irritated as he replied, 'We have some further questioning today before we leave but we shall return tomorrow with the pathologist and other officers. Then you'll all be required to make formal statements.'

Brown leaned forward, eager to get in on the act. 'And I'll need information as to where you can be contacted in future.'

'Oh, this is all so beastly!' cried Sonia, throwing down her napkin and for a moment it looked as though she was about to get to her feet and leave the room, but Locke patted her hand and she simply slumped back in her chair.

'How is Stella, Doctor? Nothing has been said about her. What is wrong with her? Is she very ill?' asked Jonquil Callow, adjusting his napkin around his neck in a vigorous fashion.

Locke looked most discomfited at this enquiry and he glanced at Wilde and then at Craddock as though seeking their help.

Before the inspector could open his mouth, Wilde said, 'I am afraid to report that Miss Bond has been the victim of a second murderous attack. Luckily, she survived but is still quite ill. Isn't that correct, Doctor?'

There was a chorus of gasps around the table.

Before Locke could respond, Callow leapt to his feet. 'My god,' he cried. 'You mean someone tried to kill that dear sweet girl?'

'Calm yourself, Mr Callow. Everything is under control...' said Craddock.

At this point. Julia gave a strangled cry and slumped back in her chair, her eyelids fluttering wildly.

To Wilde, it was clear that everything was not under control.

Locke rushed to Julia's side and within moments proclaimed that she had fainted. Gently he roused her and got her to sip a glass of water. With her husband's assistance, the doctor helped Julia from the room. Wilde followed behind.

'By Jove, this is a bloody rum do,' announced Silverside, before slurping the last of his wine. 'Christmas will never be the same again after this ghastly pantomime.' And then snatching up his dessert spoon, he added, 'Are we not going to get Christmas pudding now?'

* * *

Sometime later, Silverside tucked into a huge portion of Christmas pudding. He was the sole diner left at the table, the other guests having wandered off to their own rooms or escaped to the drawing room for a brandy and soda in search of a quiet moment, left to their own thoughts. None of them wanted conversation or to discuss the traumatic events which had unfolded in the time they had stepped over the threshold of Pelham House. Life had become a surreal nightmare; they were all waiting for it to be over.

In the meantime, Wilde had made his way down to the kitchen. The cook and one of the maids were busily washing up when he entered.

'Oh, hello, sir, were you wanting something?' Florence Daley, the cook, said, almost attempting a curtsey but failing. She wasn't used to the hallowed guests from above stairs visiting her lowly domain.

'I'm terribly sorry to bother you, especially after that splendid lunch you have given us today, but I just have a little question to ask, if I may,' said Wilde, adopting his most pleasing smile.

'Oh?' came the puzzled response. The cook dried her hands on her apron and approached Wilde. 'Was it something to do with the cranberry sauce? I always put a big dash of rum into the mix to help ease the sweetness of the berries.'

Wilde's smile widened. 'No, delicious as it was. I'll make a mental note of that. Rather, my question was to do with your knives.'

* * *

CHAPTER THIRTEEN

Lady Julia lay on the bed and her eyes opened slowly and began to focus. Markham grasped her hand. 'Are you all right, my dear?'

For a fleeting moment, her face darkened and there was a sudden ferocity in her expression and then the moment passed and her features softened. 'How stupid of me to faint,' she said. 'I am so cross with myself. I am the hostess; I should be strong.'

'It's been a trying time. It's quite understandable. Who could have thought things would turn out as they have.'

'Indeed,' she said bitterly and then looked beyond her husband to the figure of Doctor Locke standing in the shadows.

'A little nap and one of your pills, Julia, and I'm sure you'll be feeling better,' Locke said. 'What has gone on in this house is enough to put anyone under a great strain. Under the circumstances, you have been coping remarkably well.'

She closed her eyes, her features tense as she tried to contain her emotions. 'Yes, it has been terrible,' she said at length. 'You're right, doctor. I would welcome a nap. I'll take a pill later. I'd like it now if you would both leave me. I just want to be alone.' She raised her hand and in a dismissive gesture, waved them away.

'Why d'you think Wilde announced that the girl Stella was still alive?' asked Markham as the two men made their way downstairs.

'I'm not sure. Perhaps he has some plan for trapping the murderer.'

'Trapping …? What on earth do you mean?' There was a note of apprehension in Markham's voice.

'Oh, I have no way of fathoming the workings of Mr Wilde's mind. The fellow has done detective work before and he keeps his cards close to his chest.'

'God, I'll be glad when this wretched day is over.'

'Indeed,' agreed the doctor grimly. 'But that doesn't mean that this nasty business is finished with. It won't go away. I'm afraid there will be another wretched day tomorrow.'

* * *

Sometime later, after his visit to the kitchen, Rupert Wilde made his way up the same staircase and headed for Stella Bond's room. He approached it carefully and then pressed his ear to the door and listened. All seemed quiet at first and then he thought he heard some movement inside. He was sure that the girl had not suddenly come back to life and so it was clear that there was an intruder in the room. It was as he expected. Gently, he tried the handle and found to his surprise that the door began to open. It had been locked by Algernon Markham.

A thin shaft of light from the corridor arrowed into the gloomy chamber. It was like a warning beam to the person inside. It was too late. His lie that the girl had survived the murderous attack upon her had prompted the killer to return to the scene of the crime to check for themself.

Wilde heard a scuffle within and when he entered the room, it appeared to be empty apart from the body on the bed. The cover had been disturbed and the girl's vicious wounds had been exposed once more. Wilde stood motionless on the threshold, his eyes gazing around the chamber. Where on earth was the intruder? Or to be more precise, he thought, where are they hiding? He moved forward and drew back the curtains. It was already dusk and a feeble moon cast a meagre yellow beam into the room. He gave an exasperated sigh of disappointment. He listened intently for any sound but there was nothing. And no sign of the intruder. But they must be here and he was determined to seek them out. They would not leave this room without being apprehended. He dropped to his knees and peered under the bed. Again there was no one there. He next went into the small bathroom. The shower curtain which was dragged forward over the bath caught his eye. It was an ideal hiding place. He pulled back the curtain with a swift dramatic gesture, the hoops clanging noisily along the metal runners. As he did so two things happened at once. Simultaneously he experienced a range of bright multi-coloured light flashing before his eyes and at the same time he felt a violent pain at the back of his head. He turned slowly and briefly caught sight of a vague shadowy figure with an arm raised and then before he could focus on his assailant, blackness overtook him. With a muffled groan he fell unceremoniously into the bathtub.

When he regained consciousness moments later the first sensations that he became aware of were a thundering headache and the cold feel of the porcelain hard against his cheek. Slowly, he pulled himself up from his undignified posture and sat on the edge of the bathtub. He touched the back of his head and felt a bump and the tips of his fingers revealed specks of blood. He had certainly been given a good wallop. But where had his unseen assailant been hiding? The answer was revealed to him when he returned to the bedroom and observed the open door of the wardrobe. 'Blast,' he cried angrily to himself. 'What a fool I've been. Why didn't I think to look there first? It certainly would have saved me a bang on the head'. It was then that he saw that one of a pair of candle sticks was missing. This had obviously been the weapon that had given him his roaring headache and bloody scalp. No doubt his mysterious attacker had taken it away with them. Fingerprints tell tales.

Wilde moved to the bed and replaced the sheet over Stella Bond, covering both her terrible wounds and her face, providing the poor woman with some dignity. Well, he thought, my little ruse of announcing that she was still alive worked after a fashion. It had prompted someone—the killer no doubt—to come back to the room and check if this were true and to finish the job if it was. Sadly, he had been unable to establish the identity of that particular individual. They had got the better of him this time—but the game was not over yet.

* * *

Wilde returned to his room briefly to take a headache powder and down a quick slug of whisky. 'That should do the trick, ease the pain,' he muttered with a smile.

The rest of the house was rather quiet at this time. Doctor Locke and Bertram Silverside were sitting in the drawing room, both with a glass of brandy in hand, each lost in their own thoughts—each man an island. Both men wishing they were somewhere else—miles away from Pelham House. The only sound that could be heard was the ticking of the clock and the slight crackling of the logs in the grate. Jonquil Callow was in his room scribbling dark thoughts into a notebook creating a new poetic masterpiece and Julia lay quietly on her bed, staring blankly at the ceiling while her hands played frantically with a damp handkerchief. Kishen, feeling a little claustrophobic in this strange house full of tragedy had wrapped himself in his overcoat and gone out for a walk in the snow-bedecked grounds.

The only source of muted merriment in Pelham House was in the below stairs kitchen where the staff were tucking into their Christmas dinner. Boldwood was at one end of the table, Mrs Daley at the other, the two housemaids down one side, and Peter, the saturnine odd-job youth, at the other. There was little conversation but there was a sense of ease and contentment here, cocooned as it was from the dramatic trauma above stairs.

* * *

As Wilde came down the stairway to the hall, he bumped into Algernon Markham. 'Ah. "Hail to thee, blithe spirit", he said with forced jollity, patting Wilde on the back. 'I've just been summoned to my study by those two policemen fellows for questioning. I feel somewhat daunted at the prospect.' He gave a half-hearted chuckle. 'It's silly, I know, but to be honest, after all that has happened, my nerves are a bit on edge. Do come along and lend some moral support. I'd feel much more comfortable with you in the room: a friendly face and all that.'

'Happy to oblige,' said Wilde.

Markham suddenly halted in his tracks and placed an arm on Wilde's sleeve. 'I have to tell you, Rupert, that I've let it be known that Stella is dead. I was getting too many questions from the guests about her condition and that Callow fellow began insisting on seeing her. So, in the end, I informed folk individually. To be honest, most of them had guessed. Silverside even boasted that he knew 'from the off that she was a gonner.'

'How did Julia react to the news?'

Markham gave a heavy sigh. 'I'm afraid I haven't told her yet. To be honest, I've not had the courage. You saw how she reacted when you announced that

Stella had been attacked. Julia is under such a strain as it is. I'd like her to be ignorant of the truth for a little while longer. You can understand, can't you, Rupert?'

'Perfectly. But you can't keep her in the dark for much longer. She's bound to find out soon now that the others know.'

'Of course, I am aware of that. God, what a ghastly mess. I am trying desperately to keep my head above water, but I fear I am drowning.'

'I understand, but you have to stay strong for Julia's sake.' Wilde said, placing his hand on Markham's shoulder. It was all he could think to say in response.

'Yes, yes, you're right, of course. So, Rupert, shall we get this damned police business over with, eh?'

On entering the study they found that Inspector Craddock and Detective Sergeant Brown appeared to be in a jolly frame of mind. They were lounging back in their chairs chuckling merrily amongst themselves as though they were sharing a joke and had not a worry in the world. No doubt, thought Wilde, this was the result of luncheon wine and post-prandial brandy. Not ideal beverages when conducting a murder enquiry.

'Ah, Sir Algernon, here you are,' said Craddock, attempting to adopt a more sober demeanour, waving him to the interview chair.

'Actually, I am not Sir Algernon. A mere commoner, I,' Markham announced stiffly.

'But your wife is Lady Julia,' observed Brown.

'A title she inherited when she married her first husband, Lord Hereward Wainscott.'

Both policemen seemed unsure how to react to this news. Were condolences appropriate? Or congratulations on having won the fair lady? They settled for a moment's silence, during which Wilde slipped into his usual chair in the shadows.

After this pause, Craddock leaned forward towards Markham, 'I know that this is a terrible time for you, Sir, er ... Mr Markham. I mean hosting a Christmas house party where two ghastly murders have taken place, but it would be useful if you told us about your guests and your thoughts concerning what has gone on here since the...festivities began.'

Brown stifled a sarcastic laugh at the inappropriate reference to 'festivities'.

'Well, as far as I'm concerned,' Markham began expansively, 'all our guests are jolly good fellows.'

'All known by you personally?'

Markham hesitated. 'By me and, if not, then by my wife.'

'So there are some people here that you, yourself, have never met before?'

'A couple.'

'Who are they?'

'Well, there is that poet chappie, Callow. My wife met him at some literary festival and took him under her wing. She has a thing about so-called creative artists and sees it as her mission to help them develop their careers. It's a passion of hers.'

"So-called creative artists'?'

Markham wrinkled his nose as though he had detected an unpleasant smell. 'Have you read any of Callow's stuff?'

Craddock shook his head.

'Gibberish. Modern claptrap, I'm afraid. I need my poetry to rhyme and to make sense. His does neither. However, Julia thought it was striking and original. Possibly she is right.'

'What do you make of him as a person?' asked Brown.

'Can't say I have a strong opinion in that direction. He seems a little arrogant, a bit pushy maybe but in general somewhat nondescript. Possibly I'm being a little unkind, after all, I only met the fellow yesterday.'

'But the doctor, you know quite well.'

'Oh, yes. Locke. Decent chap. No quibbles about him.'

'And what of Stella Bond?' asked Wilde.

Markham stiffened at the girl's name and closed his eyes momentarily. 'Yes, poor Stella.'

'I gather that she had been a regular visitor to Pelham House in recent months?' Wilde said.

'That's right, Rupert. As you may know, she was researching the pictures in the gallery.'

'And estimating their value?'

'Well, yes. I intend to sell a few eventually to help fund certain essential repairs to the house. Some trouble with the roof...'

'Have you tried to sell any already?' Wilde asked casually.

Markham cast a searching glance at him, wondering how much he knew. Could he get away with a lie or did he have to tell the truth. He settled for a compromise. 'I haven't sold one yet,' he said.

'But you had hopes that Bertram Silverside would purchase a picture.'

Markham pulled a long face. 'I had hopes.'

'Past tense?' observed Wilde.

Markham gave a non-committal shrug of the shoulders. 'Can we move on?' he said.

'Of course,' said Craddock, leaning forward. 'Tell me what did you make of Miss Lane's charade at dinner last evening?'

'Oh, Sonia. She has always been... how shall I put it, a little extreme in her behaviour. She'll do anything to create a dramatic effect. I suppose that's the actress in her, but yesterday she really overstepped the mark. It was a cruel and thoughtless act. But having said that, I do not believe she killed her husband.'

'Then who did?' asked Brown bluntly.

'I have no idea. I wish I did.'

'I assume that you and your wife became quite friendly with Miss Bond,' said Craddock, changing tack.

'Why do you say that, Inspector?'

'Because according to you she spent some time at the house this autumn and her presence here at Christmas indicates that she was regarded as a friend rather than merely an employee.'

'Well, yes, you're right. We came to consider her as part of our little family. Neither Julia nor I have any children of our own and I suppose we both began to look on her as a kind of daughter. She brought a bit of colour and freshness into our lives. I am terribly sad and upset about her death.'

'How did your wife take the news of her demise?'

Markham looked a little surprised. 'She doesn't know the girl is dead yet.

I kept the news from Julia. She still is under the impression that Stella is ill, having survived a violent assault on her person. I didn't want to upset Julia further by telling her that the poor girl was actually dead until it was absolutely necessary. I wanted her to get through Christmas Day without any more bad news. She is under enough stress as it is without adding to it. The only thing she knows is that Stella has been the victim of another attack but has survived—as Rupert announced at lunch. That news alone upset her greatly. That is why she fainted. It was quite a blow to her.'

'As you have grown close to Stella, have you any idea why someone would want to kill her?' asked Wilde.

Markham shook his head vigorously. 'Certainly not. It's a complete mystery. Of course, we knew little of her private life really.'

'She must have had a boyfriend or lover. She was pregnant, after all.'

At this statement, Markham's whole body shuddered with emotion. 'Pregnant! I did not know that. My God, it is too terrible to contemplate. The poor, poor girl.'

'And the baby,' added Craddock. 'Are you sure that you have no idea who the father could be?'

'None whatsoever. Why should I?'

'Did Boxing Day have some special significance for her?' asked Wilde.

'Boxing Day? I don't know what you mean?'

Wilde gave a nonchalant shrug. 'Oh, it's just I thought I heard her say something to you … about the importance of Boxing Day.'

'Really?' Markham hesitated as though he was desperately trying to collect his thoughts before replying. 'Well,' he said at length, 'I know she was eager to catch the evening train back to London on the 26th and had asked me to arrange for a hire car to pick her up to take her to the station. Maybe that is what you heard.' Markham's eyes were glacial and the voice strained.

Wilde smiled indulgently. 'Yes, that was probably it.'

A blanket of awkward silence descended on the room.

A pause, then Craddock roused himself. 'Well, Mr Markham I think that will be all for now. We'll be leaving you in peace for the time being but we'll be back tomorrow. Please make sure that none of your guests attempt to leave before we return with the pathologist and other officers first thing in the morning. We shall need detailed written statements from them all before we release them.'

'Of course, I understand. If I am free to go now, I would very much like to check on the condition of my wife.'

The inspector nodded. 'Of course,' he said wearily. The day was taking its toll on his energy levels, along with the lunch and alcohol.

After his departure, Craddock turned to Wilde. 'Well now, what was all that Boxing Day stuff about?'

Wilde lit a cigarette and inhaled, blowing smoke out slowly before replying. 'It was as I'd said, I heard Stella make some comment to Algernon about Boxing Day being important.'

'Yes, but what do you understand are the implications of that?'

Wilde shifted his shoulders slightly. 'Your guess is as good as mine.'

'I don't think that is quite true.' Craddock's features darkened and there was an edge of irritation in his voice. 'I'm afraid your response does not satisfy me, Mr Wilde. I suspect that you are holding something back. I observed the glint in your eye when you asked Markham about it and your barely concealed disbelief on hearing his answer. You think he was lying. I believe you have some notion what the Boxing Day reference really means, do you not?'

Wilde shook his head and took a long pull on his cigarette. 'No,' he said softly.

'Let me impress on you, this is my case,' growled Craddock, just managing to control his temper. 'I don't want any amateur sleuths muddying the waters. Your presence here in these interviews is to assist us in reaching the truth concerning these murders. You must share your thoughts and opinions with us. It is your duty. I repeat, what was all that stuff about Boxing Day? I believe you have some theory that you're keeping to yourself.'

Wilde smiled, despite the fact that his temper had also been aroused. 'And I repeat I heard Miss Bond make some comment about Boxing Day to Algernon. It seemed important and urgent to her, but I know no more than that.'

'Very well,' Craddock responded tartly, 'but I must impress on you that you must pass on any piece of information you think might have some bearing on the investigation. I know you have a sharp mind and a bit of a track record regarding detective work, that's why I asked you to sit in on the interviews but it wasn't for you to act as a lone agent in this matter.'

Wilde nodded, but it was clear to Craddock that the gesture was of a non-committal nature. Certainly, Wilde thought, I'll tell you what I know and what I think when I believe the time is right. For example, for the moment I'm not going to reveal to you that I was attacked just now in Stella Bond's room. You're a professional policeman; you should have picked up on the possibility that the murderer would return there to check if it really was true that the girl was still alive. Wilde was aware that he was being somewhat petty in taking this stance, but he had developed a strong desire to crack this case himself and he certainly wasn't going to act as nursemaid to Craddock.

'So, we've seen everybody now except Lady Julia and your Indian fellow...' the inspector was saying.

'And Boldwood,' added Wilde.

'Yes, him too, but as a butler who, it seems, has been here since the house was built I think we can dismiss him from our list of suspects, as with Lady Julia. However, I would like to get her version of events, but,' he paused, looking at his wristwatch, 'I think she can wait until tomorrow when hopefully she'll be feeling less fragile. I reckon it's time Brown and I got off to salvage some of this day with our own families. We'll be back in the morning to take those formal statements, some chaps to take fingerprints, along with the pathologist and transport to take the bodies to the morgue in Norwich where they can be examined in detail.' He rose wearily. 'However, before we fly the nest, I'd like to ask you two fellows what your thoughts are on this case in general: motive and possible suspect for the crimes. What about you, Brown?'

The sergeant puffed out his cheeks and rolled his eyes. 'It's a clear as pea soup to me, sir. It could be that Sonia Lane is the one. She did have a reason to hate her husband, but as Mr Wilde observed would she be so stupid to get rid of him here, at a house party, especially after her performance at last night's dinner. She'd know she would become the chief suspect.'

'And what about Miss Bond, where does she—and her unborn child—fit in?' asked Wilde.

More puffing and eye rolling from Brown. 'Well, old Aubrey could have been having a fling with her, and Sonia did her in in a fit of jealousy.'

Wilde shook his head. 'That is also hard to take because we've already been informed by his wife that his amorous preferences were not towards the gentler sex. It is unlikely that he would have an affair with a young woman and make her pregnant.'

'So who's your money on, Mr Wilde?' asked Craddock. 'We seem to be running out of suspects.'

'Honestly, I don't know. I have some thoughts, of course, but they are not built on strong foundations. It's pointless to discuss them now. They are so insubstantial. I think we need to go further down the road first.'

Craddock gave a sigh. This devil was determined to play his cards close to his chest, but apart from applying a pair of thumbscrews, there was nothing he could do about it at the moment. 'Very well, but as I said, please don't keep anything from us that you consider a point of importance. You are part of this world; you know these people. Brown and I are interlopers and judging them is a hard task.'

'I'll bear that in mind,' said Wilde.

Brown gave a little cough. 'Maybe we should be making tracks, sir.'

* * *

Meanwhile, out in the grounds, Kishen was enjoying his stroll. It was cold and crisp but the nipping air pleased him. It was so fresh and invigorating after the stuffiness and claustrophobic gloom of the house. A bright full moon shone down from an azure cloudless sky like an amber spotlight, illuminating the white landscape in such a way that it resembled a stage set. He wandered down the snow-covered garden, enjoying the sensation of his feet crunching through the frozen surface of snow. The setting was far more Christmassy than the interior of Pelham House, which stood, a bleak silhouetted monolith, behind him, holding within its walls its dark murderous secrets. As he wandered nearer to the fishpond he observed soft indentations in the snow which on closer inspection appeared to be two sets of footprints which led to the edge of the pond and then made their way back to the house.

'How strange,' he muttered to himself, the words escaping as fine, minute white clouds in the night air. He followed the track of the prints to the paved edge of the pond. Its surface, silver in the moonlight, had frozen over with a thin icy sheen. However, at the point where the footprints stopped there was a small irregular hole in the ice. It was clear to Kishen that this had been created by the owner of the footprints. For what purpose, he pondered, and he knelt closer to the jagged aperture and gazed into the clear water beneath the ice. Something attracted his attention, lying down in the depths of the pond, something bright illuminated by the moonlight. Slipping off his gloves and rolling up his sleeves he bent down and dipped his hand through the glassy aperture and gave a sharp cry of surprise at the ferocity of the cold water. His hand dipped deeper seeking the bright object that he had spotted in the shallows. After a few moments, his fingers found it and gingerly he took hold of it and raised it up from its icy grave.

It was a knife. A long-bladed knife with a bone handle of the sort that was usually found in a domestic kitchen. It was clear to Kishen that this had been dropped in the pond deliberately by the owner of those footprints and quite recently, after the pond had frozen over. He gazed at the fierce serrated edge of the knife, glistening as it caught the light.

Could this be the murder weapon? His pulse began to race at the thought. Had this been used to stab Aubrey Sinclair and that poor girl Stella to death? Well, it was a distinct possibility, surely? Obviously, there was no blood on the blade and if it had been used as the weapon, the murderer would no doubt have wiped any fingerprints from the handle. One would think so, anyway. Nevertheless, it could be a vital piece of evidence. Carefully, he wrapped it in his handkerchief and placed it in the inside pocket of his overcoat, before making his way back towards the house.

As he approached the main door, he observed the two policemen emerging along with Rupert. They shook hands in a cursory fashion and then the inspector and his sergeant made their way towards a small car parked less than a hundred yards away. Kishen's first instinct was to call out to them, to rush forward and show them the treasure he had found, but he faltered. He was aware that Wilde had set his heart on unravelling this mystery and he believed, rightly or wrongly, that he should be the one who first saw his prize. Acting on this impulse, Kishen stayed back, away from the circle of light around the front door while the policemen's car revved up and disappeared noisily down the snow-covered drive.

Wilde turned and was about to re-enter the house when Kishen called out to him and rushed forward.

'Kishen?' cried Wilde peering out into the garden.

'Yes,' came the breathless reply as he stepped into the area of illumination by the door.

'What on earth are you doing out here?'

Kishen grinned. 'Investigating.'

'What?'

'I have something to show you. Something that may be connected with the killings. Is there somewhere private we can go?'

'My room of course. Come on, old chap. You intrigue me.'

* * *

Wilde examined the knife carefully. 'Well, I can say that by the design of the handle it is part of the set of knives that are kept in the kitchen here and when I checked the knife block earlier today I observed that one of them was missing. No doubt this is the one and, as you deduced, Kishen, my friend, it is most likely to be the murder weapon.'

'Disposed of in the fishpond.'

'Indeed, who would think to look there? But the more pertinent question is: who put it there?'

'The murderer.'

Wilde did not reply immediately but then said with a modicum of reserve, 'Probably.'

'Who would have access to the knife?'

Wilde gave a gentle shrug of the shoulders. 'Anyone in the house. The kitchen is not locked. It is just a matter of finding the opportunity to make away with it. I will check with Mrs Daley. She may recall when she noticed it was missing.'

'Nevertheless,' Kishen said glumly, 'it does not bring us any nearer to discovering the identity of the murderer'.

'I'm not sure. However, I agree with you that there is little hope there will be fingerprints on the handle to help in that direction. I will pass this over to Craddock and his crony in the morning, saying it was discovered after they left this evening.'

'A little lie.'

'Slightly grey rather than pure white,' chuckled Wilde.

'So what happens now?'

Wilde consulted his pocket watch. 'There is a cold buffet laid on around eight. Can't say it will be a merry gathering but I think we should go and keep our eyes and ears open to see if we can pick up anything that may prove useful in our investigations'.

Kishen beamed. 'You are really enjoying playing detective, aren't you, sir?'

Wilde raised an eyebrow. 'Who's playing?'

Chapter Fourteen

After a short nap, Rupert Wilde had showered and refreshed his wardrobe before making his way to his aunt's room. He tapped gently on the door and he was bid enter. Lady Julia was lying on the bed and gave him a smile and a wave of greeting.

'I just thought I'd come and see how you are. I know how stressful and upsetting all this has been for you personally,' he said kindly, perching on the edge of the bed.

She nodded. 'You're so right, Rupert, my dear. My nerves are in shreds,' she said. 'I've never known anything like it. I keep expecting to wake up and find it was all a horrible dream."

'You know about Stella, of course.'

Julia nodded gravely. 'Nonny finally summoned enough nerve to tell me. To be honest it wasn't so much of a shock. I suppose I knew from the start when it was announced she'd been attacked. It's just awful. Awful. We were very fond of the girl.'

'You've been very brave.'

'Sweet of you to say so, but I don't feel in the least bit brave. In fact, I feel bloody angry. I'd planned such a happy time for everyone and some foul creature has ruined it.' Her voice rose with a strained raw quality and her eyes blazed with anger.

'Take it easy, old girl.' Wilde patted her arm.

'I think I'd better have a couple of my pills, I'm sure my blood pressure is sky high. Can you get the little blue bottle from my handbag? It's on the chair over there.'

Wilde did as he was asked and snapped open the handbag. There was a blue bottle nestling at the bottom. As he retrieved it, he observed a small scrap of paper, singed at the edges with writing. He lifted this out and slipped it into his pocket. He did not quite know why he did this; it was simply an instinctive action.

He handed the pills over to his aunt who was still lying prone on the bed.

'Thank you, Rupert,' she said, pulling herself up into a sitting position. 'Now would you be a darling and get me a glass of water from the bathroom so I can take these little devils.'

'Of course.' Here was a woman who was used to servants attending to her every whim, Wilde thought as he made his way into the bathroom and looked around for a small tumbler. There was none in sight. He opened the glass-fronted cabinet over the sink and spied one there. Just as he was taking it out, he noticed another bottle of pills on a lower shelf. Swiftly he scrutinised the label: Tryptizol. He was aware of this drug as he had encountered it when he'd spent a spell in hospital during the war. Quite a number of soldiers on his ward who had been suffering from shell shock were treated with this very powerful anti-depressant. So, Dr Locke had not been quite honest when he had said that he was just treating Julia for insomnia and high blood pressure. He supposed the medic was just being diplomatic protecting his patient by suppressing that piece of information. He quickly replaced the bottle and ran some cold water into the tumbler.

'Thank you, darling,' Aunt Julia smiled as she took the glass and then popped two pills into her mouth. 'I'm not sure if they do me any good but I follow doctor's orders.'

'Quite right, too.'

'Now darling, off you go. I have to change and put on my war paint for this evening's revels. Pray God there will be no more upsets.'

'Indeed.' Wilde leaned over and kissed his aunt on the cheek. As he was leaving the room, something caught his eye on the dressing table that sent a shiver up his spine. Now that really put the cat amongst the pigeons, he thought gloomily.

*** ***

At eight o'clock the gong boomed, announcing the arrival of the cold collation in the dining room and the guests emerged from their quarters with little enthusiasm. This is a Christmas Day from Hell, thought one, while some of the others were praying for it all to be over and hoping the police would let them escape the next day. One, of course, was hoping that they would not be found out.

Originally it had been planned that there would be an evening of games—cards, billiards, and maybe charades, but no one felt at all in the mood for such frivolities under the circumstances and certainly, Lady Julia had no intention of forcing such a regime on her demoralised guests.

She fussed around them in a desperate fashion while Algernon hovered in the background unable to find any topic of conversation to impose on the others. Silverside had accosted Callow and was interrogating him about his writing. 'Do they pay you much for...poetry?' The word 'poetry' was delivered with a kind of snarling sneer.

'I don't write for money, but for the love of the art. I attempt to express my feelings and my own conception of life and living in verse form,' replied Callow with a flap of the hand.

'Really? And does that pay the rent?'

'It feeds my soul, something I suspect you know nothing of,' said the poet tartly before moving down the table and snatching up a prawn vol-au-vent.

Dr Locke sidled up to Wilde, glass in hand. Wilde assumed by the medic's relaxed features and unsteady stance that he'd had quite a number of glasses in hand already. 'Well, Sherlock, old boy,' he said in a slightly slurry voice, 'what are your deductions regarding this murder mystery of which we are all part. As helpmate to the constabulary, I suspect you know whodunnit.'

'Indeed I do,' Wilde replied flippantly. 'Now, doctor, would you like to tell me what drove you to do it? Confession is good for the soul, you know. For instance, what was your motive for the double murder, and what did you do with the weapon?'

Locke took a step backwards, his features registering shock. 'I don't know

111

what you're talking about.'

'Well, you started it, old boy.' Wilde gave him a broad smile and patted him on his back.

'That's not very funny.'

'So you are not going to confess then?'

'What rot,' Locke snarled and lurched away.

Observing this interchange, Lady Julia approached Wilde. 'What was that all about, Rupert?'

Wilde shrugged. 'Oh, something and nothing. I think the old doc has been imbibing too much medicine. Can't blame him, I suppose. Not the kind of Christmas he was expecting—nor you. I am so very sorry that things have turned out so tragic and unpleasant.'

'It's been a bloody disaster, Rupert. What I intended as a cheerful little festive house party – the sort we had before the war—has become…carnage.' She looked around at the others meandering around the room like lost souls. 'To think one of them…oh, God, it doesn't bear thinking about.'

Before Wilde could respond, Bertram Silverside made a loud announcement. 'Anyone here care for a game of billiards?'

There was silence for a moment and then Locke chimed in. 'Count me out. I'm for another brandy and then beddy-byes.' He grinned inanely.

'I'm up for a game, if that's OK with you, Julia?' said Markham.

'Of course,' she replied without much enthusiasm.

To Wilde's surprise Kishen, who had been standing quietly at the end of the buffet table, with a glass of fruit juice in hand, stepped forward and said, 'If it is all right with you chaps, I would enjoy participating also. If that is permitted.'

Silverside hesitated a moment and then pursing his lips in an exaggerated fashion said, 'I suppose so. Very well. Right, fall in, troops, and follow me to the billiard room.'

With Silverside leading the way, the three men left the room.

'At least they've found some way of entertaining themselves, unlike poor Sonia,' observed Julia. She glanced over to the fireplace where Sonia Lane sat hunched up in a large armchair nursing a drink. She looked forlorn and miserable.

'I'll go and have a word with her, try and cheer her up a little,' said Wilde. 'She'd probably welcome someone to chat to.'

'That's very kind of you, dear boy,' said Julia. 'Off you go then.'

Sonia did not look up when Wilde pulled a chair to sit beside her.

'How are you coping?' he said, knowing full well that it was a damn foolish thing to say but as he'd crossed the room this had been the only sentence that had entered his mind. In truth, he knew whatever he said would be inadequate under the circumstances. Indeed, he was also aware that trying to start up a conversation with the widow of a murdered man who was also the main suspect in the case was perhaps a futile enterprise on a hiding to nothing.

'You're an intelligent man, Mr Wilde. At least I assume you are an intelligent man, and as such, I am sure you are quite aware of how I am. How I'm feeling, deep down. However, to follow convention I will reply: I am numb, miserable, and depressed. My husband is dead. He was a man I had grown to…I won't say *hate*, that might be too incriminating…to dislike intensely but I also cannot forget that I had feelings for him once, otherwise I wouldn't have married him. So that situation leaves both my mind and my stomach in something of a turmoil. I am not comfortable in my new role as widow. I realise now that I am alone in the world. On top of all that I am suspected of carrying out the dirty deed. I am conscious that a dark cloud of scandal is hovering on the horizon waiting to envelop me and destroy my career and good name. That's how I am, Mr Wilde. Does that answer your question?'

Wilde lowered his head. 'I'm sorry. It was a bloody stupid question.'

'Do you think I did it? Stabbed my husband to death?'

'I think you may have wanted to at certain times in your relationship, but I believe that you would have arranged different circumstances in order to do it. And then… not done it. When it came to it, I don't believe you have the stomach or sufficient hatred in you to kill.'

She gave a sharp laugh. Wilde sensed that it held a faint touch of hysteria. 'So who did do it then? Who and why? Those are the questions that haunt me.'

'Surely you must have an inkling.'

She shook her head. 'It's all down to motive, isn't it? Why would anyone want to shunt Aubrey off the stage, bring the curtain down early? Do you have an answer?'

Wilde leaned forward, looking her at her keenly 'Yes, I think it was because he was in the wrong place at the wrong time,' he said, lowering his voice to a whisper.

Sonia's eyes flashed with interest.

'What do you mean?'

'He wasn't murdered in his bed, in his room, he was apparently wandering about the house in the early hours of the morning. Why? Was he going somewhere? Was he coming to your room to ask forgiveness?'

'That is a preposterous suggestion. Aubrey was too proud and in this instance too angry to even think about that. He was as glad to be rid of me as I of him.'

Wilde nodded in agreement. 'It was as I thought. So the other possibility was he was searching for something. Possibly he had been disturbed from his slumbers and had decided to investigate.'

'Disturbed from his slumbers? What on earth do you mean?'

'He was in the room next to Stella Bond's. She was attacked and stabbed. Perhaps Aubrey heard the noises from the adjoining room and went to investigate. And in doing so discovered the murderer leaving Stella's room.'

Sonia Lane's hand flew up to her mouth to stifle a cry.

'As I said: wrong place, wrong time,' said Wilde, easily. 'No complicated motive. He just had to be silenced in order to keep his mouth shut. Because he recognised the killer.'

'That is awful.'

'Murder usually is.'

'Have you told anyone else about this theory – the police?'

'Not yet – but I will do so in time. I may be wrong, of course, but I don't think I am.'

'Why are you telling me this?'

'Pardon me, I don't wish to be patronising, but I feel sorry for you and I wanted to try and ease your mind. There is no way that you will be arrested for the murder of your husband. I am convinced of your innocence, as Inspector Craddock will be when I get through with him.' Wilde smiled at her.

'You've worked this all out in your head.'

'Yes, fitting the various bits of information, pieces of the jigsaw if you like, to come up with part of the picture. The part that's missing is the one which reveals the identity of the murderer and their connection with Stella. It is my belief that she was the real targeted victim in all this. Why was *she* killed? That is the key question.'

'What an extraordinary young man you are,' she said.

'I am just a seeker after the truth.'

'Well, I thank you for what you have told me. I really appreciate your kindness. It does bring a little comfort to me.' She pressed her hand on his briefly. It was as cold as ice.

'I'm glad,' he said

'And so with that, I will wend my way to bed, hoping to get a reasonable night's sleep – one that 'knits up the ravelled sleeve of care' as some old playwright said.' She leant forward and gave Wilde a gentle, chaste kiss on his cheek before rising and leaving the room.

Wilde lit up a cigarette and smiled a self-satisfied smile. He congratulated himself on having performed a subtle double function. If, as he supposed, Sonia Lane was innocent, he had acted as a kind of ministering angel bringing some ease to her ravaged soul helping to set her mind at rest to some degree; if, on the other hand, she was guilty, he had in essence prompted her with his kind words to lower her guard, maybe making her more confident and therefore more careless. Either way, it was a useful ploy.

He sat back for a moment and surveyed the room. To his surprise, it was almost empty. Three men were off playing billiards and both Julia and Callow had performed a disappearing trick. No doubt they had sought refuge from the events of the day in their own rooms. Apart from himself, Locke was the only one left but he was slumped in an armchair at the other end of the room, his eyes closed and his hand limply holding an empty glass.

Locke hadn't struck Wilde as being much of a drinker. He certainly had consumed little the night before. What had prompted him to over-indulge this evening? He had seemed a practical, level-headed fellow. He certainly had been professional and unemotional in examining the wounds on the dead bodies. His sottish behaviour was now a little puzzling. Was it an act? Was the good doctor trying to create an impression that he was not the material from which murderers are moulded? Or had the terrible events of the past two days allowed emotion to penetrate his professional armour, leading him to find solace in alcohol? Whatever, Wilde decided to let sleeping docs lie.

He made his way to the billiard room where the game snooker was in full swing. Kishen was leaning over the table with a cue, eyeing up the ball for a shot. He glanced up as Wilde entered. 'Sorry, didn't want to put you off your stroke,' Wilde said apologetically.

'I wish you would,' boomed Silverside. 'Put him off his stroke. Your fella is a dab hand at the game. I've already lost half a crown to the scoundrel.'

Kishen smiled but said nothing.

'I learn something new about him every day,' observed Wilde. 'Just popped in to say good night, gentlemen.'

'Let's hope it is a good night tonight, not like last night, eh?' said Silverside, some of the humour fading from his voice.

'Amen to that,' observed Wilde before addressing Kishen. 'Before you hit the hay, old lad, just pop in to see me. I'd like to have a private word with you.'

'Yes, of course.'

'Good. Then I'll let you get on with your shot.'

Wearily Wilde made his way to the hall and then quickly stepped back into the shadows as he saw Doctor Locke emerge from the drawing room and move towards the staircase. He walked with a steady gait and quite swiftly, too. There was nothing about his progress that suggested tiredness or drunkenness and catching a glimpse of his face as he passed close to one of the wall lights, Wilde saw that his eyes were bright and his features alert.

On reaching his room, Wilde took another shower. Psychologically he wanted to wash away all the unpleasantness of the day. Towelled dry, he slipped on his pyjamas and silk dressing gown and lay on the bed, smoking, and thinking. In his mind, he began contemplating all that he had learned, sensed, and deduced, attempting to piece the flimsy fragments into a comprehensible mosaic along with items of factual evidence. He didn't like the picture that was forming. At first, he tried to console himself that it wasn't bound to be accurate, but he failed to convince himself. The more he pondered, the more he came to accept the inevitability of his conclusions. As a result, his stomach twisted into a tight knot. No matter how much he tried to push away the truth, it came back with greater virility, thundering in his brain. He was deep in this tangled reverie when there was a gentle tap at door.

Kishen entered. He gave a mock salute. 'Reporting for duty, sir.'

Wilde managed a faint smile. 'Take a seat and tell me all.'

Kishen did as he was asked. 'All?'

'What did you glean from those two venerable gentlemen with whom you've been playing pool and robbing them of half a crown.'

'Five shillings actually,' Kishen chuckled. 'They assumed that I was a novice. I failed to inform them that I was a whizz at billiards and pool at Oxford and won a couple of amateur championships.'

Wilde laughed heartily. 'You dog!'

'So what do you want to know?'

Wilde shrugged. 'The obvious. What did you make of your fellow competitors? Did either give off any signs, any clues that they may be a double murderer?'

'Well, neither confessed, if that's what you mean.'

'Ah, that's a pity. Certainly would have helped matters. No, what I meant was, did you learn anything that aroused your curiosity. Let's start with Silverside.'

'Oh. Oh,' cried Kishen. 'He is one big fraud. He is the head of an important motor manufacturing company and yet he behaves like a country yokel. He disguises his clever acumen with a kind of brash simplistic persona. He reminds me of that English expression: 'I wouldn't trust him as far as I could throw him'—and he's a hefty fellow.'

Wilde nodded. 'We agree on that analysis.'

'But sometimes his arrogance, which allows him to behave in such a fashion, causes him to reveal things that perhaps he would like to keep hidden.'

'Such as?'

'While I was concentrating on one of my shots tonight – taking far longer than necessary, if you catch my drift...'

'I do,' said Wilde.

'I overheard him whisper to Mr Markham that, to use his words, he would be, "hightailing it out of the house as soon as possible and there certainly would be no purchase of any of your inferior artwork or the loan that you requested. I hope that's clear Algy, old boy." Those were his exact words.'

'And how did Algy respond?'

'Strangely, with good grace. He said, "That's okay. As it happens, I don't need your charity now. My urgent need for cash has vanished." I suppose because of my lowly station and race, they conversed as though I wasn't there or I was of no importance. I am often the invisible man in the room.'

Wilde nodded. He knew exactly what Kishen meant. The arrogance of some members of the upper and middle classes regarding foreigners was abhorrent. To them, these people were of no consequence. It made Wilde's blood boil.

'Any other titbits?' he asked after a pause.

Kishen gave a gentle frown. 'I'm not quite sure. Silverside said something about being sorry to hear the "arty lass" had died and Mr Markham became a tad emotional. I thought his eyes moistened a little. "I'd rather not talk about Stella if you don't mind," he said.'

'He used her first name? Stella?'

'Yes.'

Wilde stubbed out his cigarette and yawned. 'Good work, Kishen. More clutter in the evidence bag to be shaken up and slotted in place. Now let's see what tomorrow brings.'

'The unmasking of the murderer?' said Kishen in all seriousness.

Wilde responded to this suggestion with a gloomy frown.

Chapter Fifteen

Rupert Wilde was up very early the next morning. It was still dark outside as he slipped on the jacket of his smart tweed suit and adjusted his tie. He admired his appearance in the full-length mirror on the wardrobe door. 'Mmm,' he mused, 'quite the country gent, if I do say so myself. I suppose I should have been riding to hounds in the Boxing Day hunt under normal circumstances, but Rupert, old boy, these ain't normal circumstances. Today, I corner the quarry, which brings me no joy.'

He had lain awake all night sifting through the slender pieces of evidence in his mind for the umpteenth time, constructing various scenarios that would lead him to the accurate solution of the mystery and the identity of the murderer. He was convinced that both crimes were committed by the same person and that Aubrey Sinclair had met his death purely because he encountered the killer leaving Stella Bond's room. She was the real targeted victim and so provided the key motive. But Sinclair's murder made it clear to Wilde that the killer was a desperate and probably mentally unhinged individual and it was possible they would kill again. And he knew who that person was.

Wilde considered it somewhat ironic that it had seemed more difficult to determine who the guilty party was with so few suspects in the frame. However, he felt sure he had identified the murderer. The thought of it brought a churning sensation to his stomach again. He was aware that it would be foolish to deny his convictions. He simply had to grasp the nettle.

* * *

Jonquil Callow had just finished shaving when there was a knock at his bedroom door. He frowned, catching his own uneasy reflection in the steamy shaving mirror. Who could be calling on him at this hour and more pertinently, why?

Wiping his face clean of the vestiges of shaving soap and wrapping a dressing gown around himself, he opened the door. Rupert Wilde stood before him.

'Yes?' said Callow brusquely.

'A word.'

'Now?'

Wilde nodded. 'Now.'

'What about?'

'Stella Bond.'

Callow's lips quivered nervously. 'What about her?'

'Better inside the room, old boy. It's rather a private matter.'

Reluctantly Callow stood aside and allowed Wilde to enter.

'What is this all about?'

'How long have you known Miss Bond?'

'Known her? I haven't "known her" as you put it—we only met...'

'Stop there and stop lying. It is clear to me that you and she knew each other before this wonderful Christmas house party.'

Callow gave a half-hearted chuckle. 'What on earth makes you jump to that conclusion?'

'I saw the inscription you made in that poetry book of yours: "To Cynara".'

Callow looked uneasy. 'So?'

'It's from the Ernest Dowson poem. "I have been faithful to thee, Cynara, in my fashion." Nice sentiment, but not the kind of reference one makes to a stranger, one who recognised your cufflink which had gone astray. Come now, Jonquil, you were already acquainted before you arrived at Pelham House. Lovers perhaps?'

Callow shook his head and gave a sigh of resignation. 'Passionate friends, if you like, but not lovers. Yes, you're right. I don't know why I should deny it. Certainly, we were acquainted. What does it matter now? But, as I say,

120

we were just good friends. A cliché, I know, but true. I regarded her like a close sister. We were on the same artistic wavelength. We met in the summer at some arts cocktail bash and connected quite easily. I have always been shy around women, especially attractive, intelligent women but she made things seem so easy. She seemed interested in me as a person—not as some potential lover. I would have failed that audition anyway. We were artistic bedfellows but not physical bedfellows. We dated for a while in a platonic fashion, attending concerts and art galleries. We grew close but there was nothing more than chaste kisses and affectionate hugs. I did want to take things a stage further but then suddenly she began to cool off.'

'Why was that?'

Callow sat down on the bed and gave a gentle shrug of the shoulders. 'I'm not quite sure. I suspected that there might be another man on the scene but I never caught sight of him. Perhaps she saw that my writing career wasn't going anywhere soon and she was quite ambitious. In the end, there was no great rift, we just sort of drifted apart. Until I came here I hadn't seen or heard from her for about three months.'

'Did you know she was pregnant?'

'What!' Callow's mouth gaped and he almost fell back on the bed. 'Pregnant. Are you sure?'

'Yes.'

It took Callow some moments to contain his emotions. 'By whom?'

'Well, I gather it's not you.'

'You swine! How dare you. Of course, it isn't me. Didn't I tell you there was no physical contact between Stella and I?' Callow paused in his anger and his face froze as though struck by a terrible notion. 'My God, is that why she was killed, because she was expecting a baby?'

'It is likely.'

'Then surely if you know who the father is—you have your killer.'

'Perhaps, but it may not be as straightforward as all that.'

'What on earth do you mean?'

'Nothing for now, but I ask you, if you have an inkling who committed the crime, tell me. Because I can guarantee you that when the police know of your connection with Stella, they will promote you to number one suspect.'

At this revelation, Callow's body shook with fear and he screwed up his eyes tightly as though such an action would provide him with some kind of magical escape from reality so that when he opened them he would be elsewhere, safe and far from this nightmare drama in which he had a leading role. However, on opening his eyes again some moments later and finding he was still where he had been with Rupert Wilde standing before him, deep disappointment was reflected in his strained features.

'I have no idea who killed Stella. Please believe me. I had no idea that she was pregnant and I have no notion who the father of the child could be. I swear that is the truth. I cared for the girl and I wouldn't have harmed a hair on her head. Now I would be very much obliged if you would leave me alone. Please, please go.' His voice was loud and emotional.

Wilde left the room without a word.

He made his way downstairs to the dining room in search of Boldwood. Sure enough there he was overseeing the maids preparing the table for breakfast and assuring the fire was well ablaze to heat the room to a comfortable temperature before the guests arrived.

'Ah, Boldwood, a word, if you please.'

'Certainly, sir.'

'I want a private chat with Mr Markham in his study. I don't know if he has risen from his slumbers yet, but could you inform him I shall be waiting for him at his earliest convenience.'

Boldwood's expression rarely changed, but Wilde observed a slight note of surprise at this request in those marbled features.

'Very good, sir.'

'And do tell your master that it is a matter of some urgency.'

The butler's eyes widened slightly. Now the old boy is really intrigued, thought Wilde.

'Would you like me to arrange for a fire to be lit in the study, sir?'

Wilde nodded. 'That would be excellent.'

'Leave matters to me, sir.' Boldwood gave a stiff bow and left the room.

Wilde went to the front door which was unbolted, opened it, and stood on the threshold breathing in the sharp but invigorating cold air. It freshened and revitalised his senses. He gazed across the pleasant snow-covered grounds. Everything seemed so peaceful, so still and so innocent. From the recesses of his brain, a line of poetry came to mind: 'all bloodless lay the untrodden snow.' Not quite bloodless, he mused.

With a sigh, he returned indoors and made his way to the study where he found one of the servants laying a fire in the grate. It was the dark-haired youth, the individual who had insulted Kishen on arrival.

'Won't be long, sir. Nearly finished. The fire soon gets going in this small grate,' he said cheerily, as Wilde entered. He waited until the youth had completed his task and the embryo flames, bright yellow and eager, began emerging between the crumpled newspaper and logs.

'There you are, sir,' the young lad said, wiping his hands down his apron and making his way towards the door.

'Just a moment,' said Wilde, holding up his hand. 'What is your name?'

'Peter, sir.'

Wilde strode towards him standing only inches away. 'Well, Peter, let me tell you this: if you are rude to my associate Kishen again I will make sure that you will lose your position here quicker than you can say Jack Robinson and it is quite possible I will add to your ignominy by giving you a black eye into the bargain. Is that understood?'

Peter's jaw dropped and his features paled. 'Y-Yes, s-sir,' he stuttered, backing away from Wilde.

'It is not good form to be rude about anyone's appearance or race. Only cowards do that.'

'I'm very sorry, sir. I didn't mean to...' His voice faded away.

'Good, I'm glad to hear it. Very glad that you didn't mean to...well don't again, not to Kishen or anyone else of a different colour to you. Only inferior beings stoop so low. Remember my words. Is that understood?'

'Yes, sir,'

'Good. Now off you go.'

The youth scuttled out of the room at speed.

Wilde allowed himself a gentle smile. He felt sure that young Peter would think twice before indulging in such insulting behaviour again.

Some moments later there was a gentle knock on the door. Wilde assumed it was Algernon Markham, but it turned out to be Boldwood carrying a tray containing a coffee pot, milk jug, and two cups.

'I thought you'd care for a hot drink, sir.'

Wilde beamed. 'Boldwood, you are a marvel. You think of everything.'

'I try my best, sir.'

'Indeed you do. Thank you. Just leave the tray on the desk. I'll serve myself and Mr Markham when he arrives.'

'He's on his way,' said Boldwood depositing the tray as requested.

Less than five minutes later Markham arrived. 'Good morning, Rupert. You're an early bird. What's all this about?'

Rupert did not reply immediately but proffered a cup of coffee.

'Like a coffee, Nonny?'

'What?'

'A coffee.'

'Yes, yes, I heard that,' he said taking the cup tentatively. 'What did you call me?'

'Nonny.'

Markham frowned and looked uneasy. 'Why?'

'Isn't that what some people call you? Those with whom you have a close, affectionate relationship? I heard Lady Julia address you in such a fashion last night.'

Markham nodded dumbly.

'But she wasn't the only one who called you that, was she?'

'I'm sorry, but I'm not sure what you're getting at?'

'Aren't you, Nonny? Isn't that what Stella Bond called you?'

'Stella? I don't...'

'Best not to prevaricate. You see, I know.'

'Know what?'

'Everything, old boy. I know that she was your lover.'

Markham's features froze. His eyes stared out with horror at Wilde, who for a moment thought he would collapse into a faint.

'What on earth are you talking about, man? Have you gone out of your mind?'

'Now then, Nonny, I believe that the adulterer doth protest too much. I am well aware that the truth can sometimes be painful, but there are times when it has to be faced in all its beastly glory. Sit down before you fall down. We need to talk.'

With his hand shaking, Markham placed the coffee cup and saucer on the desk and slumped into a chair.

'I don't pretend to know all the story but I believe I've got the ragged outline and now I'd like you to fill in the blanks.'

Markham said nothing.

'As I see things, when young, attractive Stella Bond came to work here, you warmed to her immediately. She was a breath of fresh air about the place. No doubt at first you saw her almost as a daughter that you never had. In fact, you said as much to me the other day. But then I guess things went further.' Wilde paused expecting a response but Markham said nothing, staring back at him stony-faced. He continued, 'I believe a romance developed between you – a genuine love affair. She, an intelligent innocent abroad, spending time in the company of a good-looking mature man of the world. It was emotional chemistry, wasn't it?'

Markham turned his gaze towards the errant flames in the grate for some time before heaving a deep emotional sigh. 'Yes,' he said, his voice emerging as a strangled, emotional whisper. 'Believe me, it wasn't planned. It just ... happened. These things do, you know. But I have to stress, it was a mutual attraction. There was no pressure on my part. We were so simpatico.'

'You had an affair.'

Markham nodded. 'It sounds so sordid put like that. In reality, it was rather wonderful and natural.'

'But then something happened. Something that blighted the romance. Harsh reality intervened. She became pregnant. You weren't expecting that were you?' There was no response again so Wilde continued. 'This unfortunate development spoiled what I suspect you viewed as a pleasant divertissement...'

'No! that is cruel. I had genuine feelings for the girl. I loved her.'

'But not enough to admit it publicly and face the resultant music.'

'Of course not. Such a thing would ruin me. I have little money of my own. It is Julia's fortune that finances our lifestyle. Without her...'

'Oh, yes, you couldn't afford to lose the bank of Julia, even though her stocks are dwindling in the post-war slump, hence your desperation to sell some of your pictures to help shore up the evaporating funds. So you dumped poor little Miss Bond. She had become an unnecessary complication. However, it wasn't quite so easy to get rid of her as you expected, was it?'

'No. She turned from a sweet loving girl into a demon.'

'Can you blame her? She had everything to lose.'

'In hindsight, I suppose not.'

'A demon, eh? A blackmailing demon.'

Markham nodded. 'She threatened...'

'She wanted money in return for her silence.'

'Yes.'

'Well, old boy, she needed money. With the prospect of a child to support and having to put her career on hold, what else could the poor girl do?'

'There's no need to be bloody sarcastic.'

'Just stating facts, Algernon. How much did she want?'

'Five thousand.'

Wilde whistled. 'The lady don't come cheap, eh? So what were you to do?'

'Well, as you can imagine there was no way I could get my hands on such a sum. That is why I became even more desperate to sell some of my pictures. I could always massage the figures for a while. Julia never took much notice of such transactions. But...'

'But you couldn't get rid of any of the paintings.'

'Not for the amount I required. So I tried the next best thing. I asked Silverside for a loan. That's why I invited him here for Christmas. I thought in jolly surroundings and with gracious hospitality, I could soften him up a bit, touch him for a loan.'

'And?'

Markham gave a wry grin. 'You've seen the man. He is tougher than an old boot. He was having none of it. The only collateral I could offer him was the paintings and he wasn't interested. "We may be on a friendly footing, Markham," he said, "but business is business and what you are offering me is a fool's deal. There is absolutely no certainty I would get my money back. Sorry old lad."'

'That put you in a bit of a spot. She wanted the cash by the time she left on Boxing Day, didn't she?'

'How the hell do you know that?'

'I overheard part of the conversation she had with you. It eventually allowed me to put two and two together and work out that she was issuing an ultimatum. The fact that she used your pet name, Nonny, and the way you reacted when you realised she was dead suggested to me there must have been some kind of intimate relationship between the two of you. What was she going to do if you didn't come up with the cash?'

'She was going to go public about our affair.'

'That certainly would throw a rather nasty spanner in the works. You must have really hated her for that.'

'Of course not. It hurt of course. She had become cold and ruthless, but if I'm honest I couldn't blame her. As I told you, I really loved her. I now acknowledge it was a foolish romance and I should have known better but sometimes the dictates of the heart overrule notions of common sense. I was devastated to learn of her death.'

'It was a convenient demise though, wasn't it?'

'What on earth do you mean?' Markham roared, his features flaming with fury. Clenching his fists he rose from the chair and took a step nearer to Wilde.

'Now is not the time for dramatics, Nonny. Knocking me down will not make anything easier for you. Quite simply Stella's death got you off the hook. With her out of the way there was no need to find five thousand pounds and there was no threat of your adulterous affair becoming public.'

'You are not suggesting that I murdered her...'

Wilde did not reply immediately, but simply stared hard at Markham. 'No,' he said at length. 'I do not believe you killed the poor girl. I accept that you had strong feelings for her and no matter how tight a corner she forced you into, I don't think you'd do such a thing. But maybe you do know who did.'

Markham shook his head vigorously. 'No, no, no. I don't. If I did I would tell you. I would shout his name from the rooftops. I want the bastard to be caught. I want him hanged!' He sank down in a chair and began to sob.

Wilde could not help but feel sorry for the man despite his despicable treatment of Stella Bond and his adulterous treachery. He was a middle-aged man who had allowed himself to be led by his passion rather than any moral compass or common sense, ignoring the dire consequences which inevitably result from such rashness and his desperation to protect the status quo. He was responsible for his own self-destruction and now he realised the full implications of his actions.

Eventually, Markham attempted to pull himself together. He dragged a white handkerchief from his pocket and dabbed his eyes. Wilde waited in silence.

'It's not just self-pity...it's for...' Markham croaked, his arms flailing aimlessly. His shoulders sank, the eyes misting once more. '...Stella...for her child, my child... everything, for the mess I've created.' He paused and gazed up at Wilde with moist eyes. 'What are you going to do?'

'Well, Inspector Craddock will have to be informed. I am afraid the truth will inevitably come to light. You will have to brace yourself for the inevitable fallout.'

'I know. God, it's going to be awful.'

More awful than you think, thought Wilde.

'My first job is to confess to Julia. She needs to know from me before she hears it from some other source. I am well aware I've behaved like an absolute cad in this matter. I've betrayed her trust and now her name will be dragged through the mud. The least I can do is tell her and beg her forgiveness—if that is possible.'

With a sudden movement, Markham rose from his chair but Wilde grabbed hold of his arm to restrain him and prevent him from leaving the room.

'No! That is the last thing you must do now.'

'Why on earth not?'

'Because she already knows.'

* * *

'I just don't believe it,' Florence Daley muttered to herself in exasperation. She looked again at the knife rack at the side of the oven. No, she wasn't mistaken. There was another knife missing. The big one yesterday and now another one had disappeared. She was sure it was there last night. What on earth was going on?

* * *

'What the devil do you mean she already knows?' roared Markham, his face flushing with anger.

'You really don't know, do you?' Wilde said with some surprise.

'What the hell are you talking about?'

'You have been bloody blind, Algernon. Somehow you foolishly thought you had been successful in keeping your furtive affair a secret from your wife. Well, I have to tell you that you failed. Failed spectacularly. Not only did Julia cotton on to what was happening but she also found out that your girlfriend was pregnant.'

Markham stared open mouthed at this revelation for some moments before he could respond. 'What! But how? We were very discreet.'

'Well wives have a way of sensing these things but I believe that she found one of the missives between you and Stella.'

'No, no. I was extremely careful. I always burned them.'

'Or thought you had.' Wilde produced a scrap of paper from his inside pocket, it was scorched around the edges.

'I took this from Julia's handbag yesterday. As you can see, the words "Nonny, I love you" are still visible. I believe that it is Stella's handwriting.'

'How do you know that?'

'I checked some of her cataloguing notes in your gallery yesterday.'

Markham snatched the scrap of paper from his grasp and stared at it in horror. 'She must have found this fragment in the grate. I was diligent in burning all the letters Stella sent me.'

'Not diligent enough, I'm afraid.'

'And the pregnancy? How did Julia find out about that?'

'Well, simple: slim girl develops a bump and despite her attempt to hide it with a sudden change from a smart to a frumpy, loose-fitting wardrobe … as I observed, women can spot these things. Pregnancy is often the outcome of a passionate illicit affair.'

'Then she has known for some time.'

'Yes.'

'And yet she never said anything.'

'That was the problem. She let it fester, eating away at her, preying on her mind until her grip on reality began to fade. You were her third husband, her last chance of marital happiness before old age came knocking hard upon her door. From Julia's perspective, you had ruined her future and so she had to do something about it.'

'What do you mean?'

'It drove her to murder.'

'Don't be…you're not trying to tell me that she was responsible for Stella's death.'

'No, I'm not trying to tell you. I *am* telling you. Possibly at first when Julia learned of your relationship with Stella, she contemplated a showdown between the three of you. No doubt she knew that the affair could not survive such an event. Julia was your security, your lodestone of respectability. She was fully aware that you needed her and no doubt she believed that you would return to her with your tail between your legs having given Stella the brush off. However, when Julia learned of the pregnancy - a Markham bastard appearing on the scene – this introduced another element into this sordid equation. Things couldn't be covered up so easily. Now she was not certain which way your loyalties would lie. Would you ride off into the sunset with your young lover and your child leaving her alone? She certainly couldn't be sure that you'd stay with her. And even if you did… how could she face the world with her husband having fathered an illegitimate child with a woman half his age? To her fevered mind, there could only be one solution. The girl must die. When you had the brass nerve to invite her here for Christmas, she saw that this would be the ideal opportunity to do away with her.'

Markham shook his head vigorously. 'No. No. No. This is a fantasy. You must be wrong. Not Julia.'

'But she's not Julia anymore—not the old Julia. Even I could see that. The stress of this situation has driven her over the brink. She was already unwell and then the discovery of your infidelity and its disastrous outcome edged her further towards madness. She saw only one solution: the girl and her child must die. That was the only way to retain her status quo. Julia has grown cunning, deceitful, and vicious. Have you not noticed her rapid mood swings? The anti-depressant pills she is dosing herself with and her apparent calmness during the maelstrom of events that have taken place over the last few days?'

'This can't be true. It's all a fabrication of your imagination, Wilde. I don't know what you hope to achieve with this cock and bull story.'

'Stop for a minute, man. Think and consider all the points I've mentioned. They fit the facts. One other thing—when I went to Stella's room after I had announced that she had been attacked but was still alive, I discovered an intruder in the room. Unfortunately, I did not get a glimpse of them because they slugged me on the head with one of a pair of candlesticks, which they took away with them. I discovered it later in Julia's bedroom.'

'But she's your aunt for God's sake...!'

'I know! I know! It pains me to believe it. But despite my feelings, I can't ignore the facts. It's terrible but it's true.'

'Well, *I* refuse to believe it.'

'I understand your reluctance but trust me. Would I invent such a story or express such an opinion unless I was absolutely certain?'

'What ... what if I were to tell you that it was me? I killed Stella and that blasted playwright.'

Wilde shook his head. 'Not a credible confession, I'm afraid. I saw your reaction when we discovered Stella's body. You were devastated and shocked as we all were. I know this is very hard and difficult for you ...'

'Oh, do you! How bloody perceptive of you, standing there coolly, telling me my wife is a double murderer and my whole world is crumbling around me.' He turned suddenly and made a dash for the door. 'I must talk to Julia,' he cried.

Wilde leapt forward, grabbing his arm, restraining him. 'No, you must not speak to her or raise her suspicions…not until the police arrive and arrest her. Who knows what she will do if she realises the truth is known.'

'You bastard!' Markham roared in anger, thrusting Wilde aside. 'You can't tell me what to do.' With a desperate cry he suddenly lashed out with his fist, hitting Wilde squarely on the chin, sending him crashing to the floor. In an instant, Markham was at the door, where he retrieved the key from the lock.

Before Wilde could get to his feet, Markham had slammed the door shut behind him, Wilde heard him lock it from the outside.

'Markham, don't be a fool,' he bellowed, but he knew his words were futile.

Chapter Sixteen

Kishen was returning from an early walk around the grounds when he encountered Lady Julia emerging from the house wrapped in a large fur coat.

'Good morning,' he said politely, giving a slight bow. 'Taking a morning constitutional?'

Julia looked distracted and uncertain how to respond to this innocuous statement. She just nodded vaguely and moved away swiftly without a word around the far side of the house.

Kishen gave a gentle shrug, accepting that the ways of the British aristocracy would always puzzle him. On entering the house, just as he was about to mount the stairs and return to his room, he heard a strange rumbling noise emanating from down the corridor that led to Markham's study. He stood for a moment and listened. The noise continued. Kishen decided to investigate. Approaching the study, it sounded as though someone was inside hammering on the door and calling out for help. As he grew closer, he recognised Wilde's voice. Observing the key in the lock he turned it and opened the door. Wilde almost fell into his arms.

'Good man,' cried Wilde, his face flushed from his exertions.

'What is going on?'

'No time to explain. Have you seen Algernon Markham just now?'

Kishen shook his head.

'Damn. Then we must get to Julia's room post-haste.'

Wilde ran at full pelt along the corridor and up the stairs with Kishen following close behind. The door to Julia's room was open. On entering,

Wilde froze as he gazed at the sight that met his eyes. There on the floor by the bed was the body of Algernon Markham. He was lying on his back, a kitchen knife embedded in his chest. The wide, staring, lifeless eyes clearly indicated that he was dead.

'My God,' muttered Wilde, bending down by the body and feeling for a pulse just to make sure he was correct in his assumption. There was none.

'Great heavens, what is going on?' asked Kishen.

'It's Julia. She's the murderer.'

'Your aunt? She did this …?' Kishen pointed at the corpse on the floor, his eyes wide with shock. 'And the others?'

'Yes. I'm afraid so.'

'My goodness! But why? I don't understand.'

'Too complicated to discuss now. We must find her quickly. She's obviously out of her mind and who knows what further mayhem she'll cause unless we catch her.'

'I've just seen her.'

Wilde jumped to his feet. 'Where?'

'She was leaving the house. I'd been for a walk in the grounds and as I came back, I saw her outside…'

Wilde was out of the room before Kishen could finish the sentence. He raced down the steps, through the hall, and out onto the portico where, with his hand shielding his eyes, he scanned the grounds looking for a figure, the figure of Lady Julia. He saw none, but he did notice a set of tyre tracks emerging from the side of the house in the virgin snow. They led down towards the gates.

'She's made a bolt for it,' he muttered to himself, before hurrying back into the house, almost colliding with Kishen.

'Did you see her?' he asked.

'No.'

'What now?'

'Just come with me,' came the terse reply as Wilde hurried to the dining room. As he suspected, Boldwood was supervising the final touches to the breakfast arrangements. He raised a concerned eyebrow as Wilde burst into the room and approached him at speed.

'Her ladyship's car. What make is it?'

For a brief moment, the butler seemed a little taken aback by this sudden abrupt query.

'Oh, it's rather a sporty item, sir.'

'Yes, yes but what make!'

Boldwood had to think for a moment before he was able to answer. 'It's a Morgan-Adler Carette in light blue.'

'Thank you. Come on, Kishen, we've got a chase on our hands.'

* * *

Less than five minutes later, with Wilde at the wheel and Kishen in the passenger seat, the little red roadster roared down the drive of Pelham House onto the snow-covered road. 'God knows where Julia is going. Her mind isn't working clearly so I suspect she doesn't even know herself, but we've got to catch up with her before she is able to go to ground.'

'She really did commit all those murders?' Kishen said, still finding it hard to accept Wilde's assertion.

'I am afraid so.'

'The poor woman.'

Wilde turned briefly to his passenger. 'A very strange but kind observation.'

'Well, Rupert, as you intimated, she is not in her right mind. No doubt her right mind would be appalled at her actions.'

'Of course, you are correct, but I am afraid the law will take rather a dim view of it all. My concern now is to get to her before she does any more hurt to others or, indeed, to herself. In her current frame of mind, there is no saying what she might do. If she gets to Norwich she could easily lose us there.'

Kishen was about to respond to this observation but instead he closed his eyes as the car skidded wildly round the narrow bend in the road, the back wheels riding up into the grass verge. 'Must we go so fast? You never know what is coming along in the opposite direction.'

'I have to go fast in order to catch up with Julia. Besides it is Boxing Day, so there will be little traffic about.'

Kishen raised his eyes to the heavens. 'Let us pray so.'

Wilde drove on, increasing his speed slightly. He was well aware that he was being somewhat reckless manoeuvring the car in this fashion along the narrow winding roads in these snowy conditions but needs must…

Meanwhile, Kishen intermittently closed his eyes or gripped the sides of his seat anticipating a crash at any moment.

As they breasted the curve of a hill and began to career downwards into the valley, Wilde spotted a moving speck on the road ahead climbing up out of the other side. 'That may be her. If so, we're catching up,' observed Wilde, pressing his foot a little harder on the accelerator.

* * *

Julia Markham was driving like an automaton. Her mind was free of all thought and her control of the car was purely mechanical. All she knew was that she had to escape. To get away from everything dark and unpleasant. Where to—she had no notion. Her memory was in rags and tatters. She had no real concept of who she was or her past history. That part of her conscious mind had shut down and was a clouded blank. At least there was some comfort in the blurry whiteness that skimmed past her and the winding ribbon of road which twisted and turned at will. It was hypnotic and strangely soothing. And in the dark recesses of her mind, she knew that she was in great need of soothing. She caught a glimpse of her reflection in the driving mirror and smiled. There she was gazing back at herself, a young woman again, barely twenty with blonde ringlets surrounding her glowing features. She gave a sigh of contentment as she admired her youth and beauty. 'Age cannot wither her,' she mouthed softly before beginning to hum a melody from her lost youth. As Julia drove on contentedly, she was completely unaware that a red roadster was tailing her and gaining ground.

* * *

A few miles ahead in the opposite direction, Inspector Craddock and Sergeant Brown were making their way to Pelham House once more. In the back seat of the car was Horace Walters, the pathologist, who, suffering from a bad cold, was not best pleased to be dragged from his warm home on Boxing Day to deal with two dead bodies in the wilds of the countryside. Behind Craddock's car was the mortuary wagon which would take the bodies from Pelham House to the morgue in Norwich for examination by the forensic team.

Craddock was driving at a steady speed, partly because he did not like these snowy conditions, which he considered potentially treacherous, and partly because his head was thumping with a giant headache—the result of staying up too late and consuming too much alcohol the night before. It had been his compensation for having spent most of Christmas Day in the gloomy confines of Pelham House. It had not been the Christmas Day he had planned for nor would ever want to experience again. Now here he was giving up his Boxing Day to return to that blasted gloomy mausoleum. I wonder, he thought sarcastically, if anyone else has been stabbed to death overnight. That's all I need: another dead body.

By contrast, Sergeant Brown was irritatingly cheerful. 'I'm hoping that one of these blighters slips up badly when they are making their formal statements,' he was saying. 'It does happen. The guilty ones gain in confidence and without realising it they give the game away, thus pulling the rug from under their own feet and incriminating themselves. Don't you agree, sir?'

Craddock responded with a non-committal grunt.

Their car took a sharp left-hand bend and then the wheels slithered on the ice and began to coast and then spin slowly. Craddock swung the steering wheel wildly in an attempt to halt the skid but to no avail. The car was gently skating in a sideways direction. Slamming his foot on the brake also had no effect on the vehicle's trajectory. It was as though some giant invisible hand was guiding its progress. Gradually the car slithered to a halt, coming to rest, lying directly across the narrow roadway. The driver of the mortuary wagon behind observing this, braked heavily but this action had only minimal effect and slowly but with a hypnotic inevitability, the wagon ran gently into the side of Craddock's car pushing it another six feet down the road before both vehicles came to a slithering halt. The thoroughfare was now completely blocked. With some effort Craddock, muttering oaths under his breath, clambered out of the car and promptly slipped on the ice and crashed to the ground, his trilby hat flying in the process. This time he swore loudly in a most violent fashion.

* * *

Julia had not noticed how cold the car was becoming and that the windscreen was slowly steaming up. Her vision was blurred as though she were driving in a fog. She found herself leaning forward closer to the glass in order to see out clearly. Although it was still early morning, the sky was dark with an even greyness that seemed to threaten further snow. Then suddenly through the misted screen she saw ahead of her what looked like a car and a large blue van straddled across the road directly in front of her. It took her a few seconds to comprehend that this wasn't some snow-induced mirage but very real. On realising this, her heart skipped a beat and, briefly, reality fought its way back into her mind. She let out a scream in panic and gripping the steering wheel hard, she swung it to the right, hoping to direct the car away from these obstacles. She had not reasoned that such an action would take her off the road. With the squeal of protesting tyres, the car shuddered violently as it reared up, mounting the high uneven grass verge. Julia was flung back in her seat, her hands wrenched from the steering wheel as the car carried on moving forward. She screamed at first as the vehicle rolled on for a few feet and then began to tumble down the side of the deep gully beyond.

Inside, her body was flung about from one side of the cab to the other as the car rocked violently in its descent. Julia Markham was exhilarated by the sense of freedom this gave her. Suddenly she began laughing. And then her face crashed with great force into the windscreen. The laughter died, and as blood seeped from her mouth, she lost consciousness.

With a loud groan of twisting metal, the small car turned over onto its roof. Finally, it rolled further down the steep incline, crashing into a line of rocks at the base of the gully, the bonnet buckling like a concertina on impact. In the sudden stillness, Julia stirred but she was too weak to move.

Craddock and Brown ran forward to the top of the gully, just in time to see fire burst from the damaged bonnet and very quickly engulf the rest of the motor car. There was one muffled scream from inside and then silence apart from the fierce roar of the voracious flames.

The policemen stared in shock and horror, but did not move, standing as still as statues surveying the terrible scene before them. It was clear that there was no hope of rescuing the driver from the inferno. Then their attention was taken by the arrival of another motor car. The two occupants emerged and Craddock recognised them as Rupert Wilde and his assistant, the Indian fellow, Kishen.

For a moment no one spoke.

Wilde moved to the edge of the gully and gazed down at the wrecked vehicle, the flames now subsiding, leaving a blackened shell, like a rough charcoal sketch against the whiteness of the snow. There was no mistake, it was the remains of a light blue Morgan-Adler Carette: his aunt's car.

Wilde shook his head in disbelief and he felt an ache in his stomach.

'What on earth are you doing out here?' asked Craddock.

An ashen-faced Wilde turned to face the Inspector who thought he saw a tear fall down the young man's face.

'It's a long story and more fitting to be told in a warmer place than this.'

Chapter Seventeen

Some hours later, Wilde, Kishen, Inspector Craddock, and Sergeant Brown along with Boldwood were sitting near the fire in the drawing room of Pelham House. Each had a drink and each wore a grim expression. They were now the only ones left in the house, apart from the servants. With a great sense of relief Doctor Locke, Jonquil Callow, and Bertie Silverside had departed. 'Released into the wild', as Brown had phrased it. They had been told that their presence and statements were no longer required, they were free to go, and that the case was closed. They may have been intrigued by this sudden turn of events but were too eager to leave to request any explanations. 'We'll read about it all in the papers,' observed Bertie Silverside. 'The full gory details no doubt. They're always slow press days after Christmas.'

The departure of the guests cast an even gloomier pall over this blighted house. The Christmas tree, its lights now extinguished, stood in the hall like a dark arboreal phantom. The shadows which stretched along the corridors and invaded the empty chambers seemed darker and more invasive than ever as though they were about to claim the house as theirs at last.

Inspector Craddock leaned nearer to the fire and sighed. 'It's been a hell of a day,' he observed, expressing the thoughts of all. 'Well, two days really. Quite dramatic and no doubt especially traumatic for you, Mr Wilde.'

Wilde did not reply. Somehow he felt he was not fully there in the room with these people. Part of him was somewhere else – a quiet, remote place, away from the mayhem and pain. Life no longer seemed in focus and he was losing the facility to engage with reality. He knew what he had experienced hadn't been a dream; he just wished it was.

Kishen leaned forward and gently shook Wilde's arm. 'Are you all right, Rupert?' he said softly.

With a Herculean effort, Wilde tried to pull himself together. He knew he had to shake off this emotional malaise which was the result of his mixed emotions: he was tired, distressed, and strangely angry. He gave Kishen a brief nod in response.

'If you are up to it, Mr Wilde,' Craddock was saying, 'I'd appreciate your version of the events that have taken place here. I need to get things right for my report.'

Brown leaned forward, poised with pencil over his notepad.

It was some moments before Wilde responded. 'You want my story?'

'Well, yes. You hold the key to the whole sorry business.'

'I suppose I do,' he said with a sigh of resignation. 'It is not a pretty tale, I'm afraid, but I understand that it is one that has to be told for the record at least.'

'Indeed,' said Craddock. 'I have picked some of the structure of what happened but we need to know all the details.'

Wilde took a gulp of brandy. It burnt his throat and helped clear his mind and sharpen his thoughts. 'Certainly, we all need to know the truth and that is why I have invited Boldwood here to join us. He has been the lynchpin that has ordered this household for many years and will need to carry on doing so for some time to come until all the business of wills and estate affairs are sorted out.' He turned his gaze towards the old butler and gave him a brief warm smile. 'As you know, Boldwood, my dear fellow, this old pile has no real master or mistress at present. You must assume charge for the time being.'

'I will do my best, Master Wilde.'

'This has been quite a Christmas, Mr Wilde,' said Craddock, leaning forward in his chair. 'Three murders and another corpse in a road crash to add to the total. So please tell us what the hell has been going on? Unravel it all for us.'

'It is not an easy story for me to relate. I am still coming to terms with the fact that my aunt, my dear mother's sister, was the perpetrator of the vicious murders that took place under this roof. What I am about to say is merely my understanding of things. I'm sure that further investigations will cross all the t's and dot all the i's, but what I'm about to relate is, I believe, the basic truth of this awful affair.'

He paused. No one spoke for a time, only the crackling of the logs in the grate broke the silence.

Wilde took another drink of brandy before continuing. 'It is clear to me that Julia's mental health has been in decline for some time. No doubt the stress of maintaining Pelham House was a contributing factor; but when she discovered that her husband was having an affair with the young woman Stella Bond, who was spending time here working in the picture gallery, her mental state deteriorated quickly. Her suspicions were raised when Algernon was spending so much time with Stella and then she found the fragment of one of her love letters to her husband in the grate in his study. This, I reckon, triggered her descent into a kind of madness. Algernon was her third husband. She couldn't lose him, not at her time of life. Initially, no doubt, she felt she could break up this affair and return to the old status quo. However, the final straw, as we might say, was when she learned that Stella was expecting a child—Algernon's. To her an illicit affair was one thing, but a bastard child was a far more damning matter. To Julia, it was a bridge too far. No doubt the anguish she felt drove her further towards the edge of insanity. I believe that in her fevered mind she thought that the only way to deal with this problem, to alleviate the pain and banish it from her life, was to kill the girl and her baby. She saw this Christmas gathering as the ideal time to do it. With a house full of guests, who would consider the hostess as the culprit?'

'She acquired the murder weapon from her own kitchen and she later disposed of it in the garden pond. By this time, I reckon she was living in a half-world of reality, her mania and her pills sustaining her. The fact that she had drifted into a kind of uncontrolled madness is clear from her desperate murder of Aubrey Sinclair, who had the misfortune to see her leaving Stella's room after she had killed the poor girl. He recognised her of course and in her heightened state she knew she had to kill him so that he couldn't expose her. It must have been that nothing was quite real to her anymore, despite the fact that part of her brain was cunning enough to allow her to maintain a reasonably sane and restrained public persona. I must confess I had my doubts about her sanity at the close of Christmas Day, but I found it hard to accept because…well because she was my aunt. My own flesh and …I had known her all of my life.'

At this point Wilde paused and turned his back on the others, his body shuddering with emotion. He was still only allowing the terrible truth to drip feed into his consciousness. In assembling his thoughts in this way, he was facing the stark reality of the tragedy.

After an awkward pause, Sergeant Brown piped up. 'What I don't understand is why she killed her husband.'

Slowly Wilde turned round again. His eyes were moist but he had regained control of his emotions. 'I am sure some clever psychiatrist would explain the reason in a cold and clinical manner. All I can assume is that when he came to her room ready to confess his infidelities and beg her forgiveness she just erupted in fury. Here was the man who was the source of all her pain and distress now admitting to her his failings and weakness, begging for mercy. He was the man who had destroyed her life. It must have been too much for her. She just lashed out …'

Wilde drained his glass of brandy.

'The end was ghastly but perhaps it was for the best,' observed Craddock. 'She would either have gone to the gallows or ended her life in some grim institution for the insane.'

Wilde could only nod in silent agreement.

'All those lives lost. For what?' said Kishen, placing his hand on Wilde's shoulder.

Chapter Eighteen

New Year's Eve 1919

Rupert Wilde held up a glass of champagne close to his face, staring intently at the shimmering bubbles. 'They are lively little things, these bubbles, dancing about without a care in the world.'

Kishen, who was sitting opposite him in Wilde's flat, raised up his glass of lemonade in a similar fashion and smiled. 'My bubbles are lively, too, but not as intoxicating.'

Wilde chuckled. 'You don't know what you're missing,' he observed.

'Maybe, but I reckon what you've never known you do not miss.'

'You have a sagacity beyond your years, old lad. I can always rely on you to come up with a nugget of wisdom.'

Before Kishen could reply, there came the booming sound of Big Ben striking midnight. Both men moved to the window and Wilde opened it, allowing the chill night air to invade the room. Across the darkened city the chimes brought in a new year and a new decade. In the street below, a group of revellers was celebrating the occasion in their own jolly inebriated fashion.

Wilde smiled and then closed the window. 'I shall not be sad to see the back of the old year,' he murmured.

'Indeed,' agreed Kishen. 'It has been a painful one for you and a family tragedy hurts the most.'

'Yes. I hope you don't think I am callous when I say that I intend to blank that dreadful Pelham House business from my memory.'

'Of course not. You are right to do so. It is the healthiest option. There is no point in dwelling on the unhappy incidents of the past, ones that you cannot alter. It is best to cast them from your mind and move on.'

'My thoughts exactly. I am determined that 1920 sees a new start for me and hopefully a brighter future.'

'I'll drink to that,' said Kishen beaming.

'So will I. You in lemonade, me in champers'. The two men clinked glasses and smiled.

Chapter Nineteen

As far as new Year's resolutions go, thought Rupert Wilde, this was a significant one. If there was anything positive that he could retrieve from the dreadful business at Pelham House it was his growing acumen as a detective. Despite the appalling outcome of the affair, he believed that he had acquitted himself well as a perceptive sleuth as he had done when he'd assisted his old friend, Inspector Johnny Ferguson, in solving the theft of Lady Dobney's diamond tiara. And so he finally admitted to himself that he had a modicum of talent for detective work—if nothing else. Therefore, he intended to put this skill to use in a professional manner.

* * *

In January 1920 the following advertisement appeared in the personal column of all the major London newspapers:

Mysteries Unravelled
Problems Solved
Rupert Wilde
Private Investigator
1A Chancery Court, Kensington
Telephone: KEN 221

'Casting your bread on the waters, eh?' observed Kishen on reading the notice.

Wilde grinned. 'Who knows? All I may get is just soggy bread'.

Kishen chuckled, his eyes flashing with merriment. Unseen by Wilde, his assistant had the fingers crossed on both hands.

* * *

Towards the end of the month on a dreary, rain-soaked morning, Rupert Wilde's doorbell rang furiously. Kishen was out of the flat engaged in shopping for provisions, so Wilde answered the door himself. Standing on the threshold was a young woman, wet through to the skin, her dark hair plastered to her face. She was clutching a folded newspaper in her hand, which Wilde could see bore his advertisement.

'Are you Rupert Wilde?' she asked, breathlessly. 'Mysteries unravelled?'

'I am.'

She gave a huge sigh of relief. 'Thank heavens. I need your help desperately...'

About the Author

David Stuart Davies is an author, playwright, and editor. He has written nine Sherlock Holmes novels and *Starring Sherlock Holmes,* which details the film career of the famous sleuth. He has also created several detective series set variously in London during World War II, New York in the 1930s, and in 1980s Yorkshire. His non-fiction work includes *Bending the Willow: Jeremy Brett as Sherlock Holmes*, which is regarded as the definitive work on the subject.

Currently, he is the general contributing editor for Wordsworth Editions Mystery & Supernatural series. He is a Baker Street Irregular, and a member of the Crime Writers' Association (he edited their monthly magazine *Red Herrings* for twenty years) and The Detection Club. He has given talks and dramatic presentations on crime fiction and his collections of ghost stories at various literary festivals, libraries, and conferences as well as on the Queen Mary II.

SOCIAL MEDIA HANDLES:

Twitter: @DStuartDavies

AUTHOR WEBSITE:
davidstuartdavies.co.uk

Also by David Stuart Davies

SHERLOCK HOLMES NOVELS:

Sherlock Holmes & the Hentzau Affair

The Tangled Skein

The Veiled Detective

The Shadow of the Rat

The Scroll of the Dead

The Devil's Promise

The Ripper Legacy

The Instrument of Death

Revenge from the Grave

JOHNNY HAWKE NOVELS:

Forests of the Night

Comes the Dark

Without Conscience

Requiem for a Dummy

The Darkness of Death

A Taste for Blood

Spiral of Lies

THE PAUL SNOW TRILOGY:

Brothers in Blood

Innocent Blood

Blood Rites

OTHER NOVELS

Oliver Twist and the Mystery of Throate Manor

The Scarlet Coven

The Darkness Rising

SUPERNATURAL COLLECTIONS:

The Halloween Mask

In the Shadows

NON-FICTION:

Holmes of the Movies

Starring Sherlock Holmes

Bending the Willow: Jeremy Brett as Sherlock Holmes

The Sherlock Holmes Book (co-edited with Barry Forshaw)